Christmas in Ashton

Kendall H. Williams

Christmas in Ashton
By Kendall H. Williams
First Edition, December 2013

ISBN: 978-0615933504

Copyright 2013
Kendall H. Williams Publications; Pleasant Grove, Utah
kendall_williams16@yahoo.com

All poetry in this book is composed by the author, Kendall H. Williams.

Cover painting, "Bradford Inn," by Julie Lynch.
J.A.L.S@icloud.com

Cover design and layout by Bradley Jackman of Shoebox Genealogy.
www.ShoeboxGenealogy.com

Christmas in Ashton

Kendall H. Williams

Kendall H. Williams Publications

Pleasant Grove, Utah

Author's Dedication:

For my family

Author's Note:

In 1998 I spent Christmas in Stowe, Vermont, and became acquainted with several wonderful people who were brought together by remarkable circumstances. I was captivated by their history and I dug deeper, asking an endless list of questions and eventually researching their ancestry. The family freely shared with me their memories, records, and journals, which together seemed to tell an unbelievable tale. As I began to piece the events together, I knew it was a story that needed to be told. With the permission of those persons involved, I share with you their story: Christmas in Ashton.

Chapter One

Winchester

Friday, December 15, 1950

"Yes, I'll take it, and I'll have heels, gloves, and a hat to match."

The young lady stood alone in front of the full-frame mirror, admiring the fashionable suit that she held up to her.

"Put it on my account," she added with a big smile as she pictured herself wearing the suit to church on Christmas Eve.

Bonnie Pratt's was one of the more fashionable women's boutiques in Boston, Massachusetts. No one was in the store, except for Laura Winchester. The sign in the boutique's window read: "Closed." Laura neatly put the two-piece suit back on its hanger and returned it to a rack. She bit her lower lip, and her smile faded. Laura's face turned somber. Reality set in, and she resumed her cleaning duties: dusting, washing, and waxing the floor. She worked at Bonnie Pratt's every evening after completing a full day's work as a sales clerk at Fitzgerald's 5 & 10¢ store across the street.

George Fitzgerald was too cheap to hire someone to clean his establishment. Laura was his only employee, and he expected her to clean the store, stock the shelves, and wait on customers.

Laura arrived an hour early every morning to make the store presentable. She opened the shop precisely at nine o'clock in the morning, even though very few customers frequented the premises before ten.

Mr. Fitzgerald would wander in at noon and leave promptly at four o'clock. He was a short, crusty-looking man, and rather plump. A bachelor of Irish extraction, he always appeared to have slept in his clothing. Laura closed the store at six o'clock, even though all the other stores in the area closed at five. George Fitzgerald wanted to make every cent possible.

This December, Fitzgerald's, like the other stores in the area, would stay open each evening through December 23. While the other stores were closing at nine o'clock at night, Fitzgerald's would remain open an additional thirty minutes. Although her workday was greatly extended, Laura gladly worked the extra hours because she needed the additional income. She had no breaks and was expected to eat her meager lunch on the premises. That was fine with her, though, since she could afford only an apple and a peanut butter and jelly sandwich, which she brought with her each day.

With the exception of December, Laura left her small apartment at seven thirty each morning and arrived home at eight thirty each evening. During December, she would immediately fall into bed upon entering her apartment at midnight. Six days a week, she labored. Rent, utilities, and food consumed most of Laura's meager salary. The cleaning job at the dress boutique made it possible to compensate Laura's neighbor, Mrs. Nelson, who tended Laura's two small children while Laura was working.

Laura Winchester, full-time sales clerk and part-time cleaning woman, enjoyed little happiness, except for her children: five-year-old Sara Elizabeth and seven-year-old Samuel William Winchester Jr. There was little need for the "Junior" now, as Samuel Sr. was killed in action during the final days of World War II.

Life had not always been difficult for Laura. She grew up

in St. Albans, Vermont. While other families suffered during the Great Depression, her father, a policeman, was always employed.

After graduating from high school in 1939, Laura went to Boston to live with an older sister. She obtained employment as a waitress in a small restaurant in Cambridge, near Harvard University. That was where she met Samuel. He was an only child whose parents were both deceased. Laura and Samuel were married New Year's Day, 1941.

Samuel completed his degree in advertising that spring and was offered a good position with one of Boston's more affluent advertising agencies. Samuel and Laura celebrated by buying a new Plymouth. (Laura still had that Plymouth in 1950 but rarely used it, except for taking the children on rare Sunday drives and even rarer trips to visit her parents in Vermont.)

In 1942, Samuel enlisted in the US Army but was not shipped overseas until June 1944. He never lived to see his daughter, Sara, who was born February 24, 1945. Captain Winchester was killed in action in July 1945 as the Third Army was pushing toward Berlin.

Christmas 1950 was going to be special! Christmas Day would fall on a Monday. Laura was leaving after morning worship services on Christmas Eve to join her parents in Vermont. George Fitzgerald, in a rare mood of generosity, had promised her the day after Christmas off—with pay.

Unlike the average wage earner, Laura was never allowed to take breaks. However, she wanted to make this Christmas special for her children. So for the past three months, Laura had begged Mr. Fitzgerald to give her a thirty-minute break every other Saturday. He would moan and groan, but he always relented.

It took Laura exactly ten minutes, walking briskly, to get to Sullivan's Toy Shop, where she had her children's Christmas presents on layaway. The few dollars she gave Sullivan's every two weeks were difficult for Laura to spare. After each payment was made, she left the store with a big grin of satisfaction. This brought her a rare moment of exhilaration. This sacrifice was for her children!

Saturday, December 23, 1950

It was past noon, and Laura became fidgety. The one thing that she could normally count on with Mr. Fitzgerald was that he would arrive at noon and leave at four o'clock. When the clock struck two and there still was no sign of him, Laura became extremely nervous. Since it was the last shopping day before Christmas, the 5 & 10¢ store was especially busy, and Laura desperately needed Fitzgerald's help. She needed him to mind the store so she could take a break to make her final payment at Sullivan's and pick up her children's Christmas presents.

Laura telephoned Fitzgerald's house. No answer. Thinking she may have misdialed, she tried a second time. Still no answer.

"Don't panic," she said softly to herself. "He will come."

A customer in the sewing department was trying to get Laura's attention. Others were waiting at the register. She had no choice but to help those at the register. Inside, she was a bundle of nerves. As one customer would exit the store, two more would come in.

Three o'clock... four o'clock... five o'clock... six o'clock. Laura began to feel anger toward Fitzgerald and disdain for her customers. She tried not to show her displeasure, but she began to be short with the shoppers.

"What do you want?" she snapped at a young boy who was trying to get her attention. This perturbed his mother, who dropped her armload of figurines and picture frames, grabbed her son, and left the store in a huff. No one else dared ask Laura a question as she cleaned up the broken figurines and glass. Her loss of control released some of the tension within her.

Laura thought to herself: *Why should I care?* This is Fitzgerald's store. I am only one person, and I cannot handle all these people alone. It is his problem, not mine.

The line at the register became longer. Several customers made it a point to display their intolerance of waiting by rudely slamming their desired purchases down on the counter and coldly stomping out of the store. However, Laura maintained control and politely spoke to those waiting. "I am doing the best I can. Please, be patient. I will get to each of you as soon as possible."

Seven o'clock. Shoppers were everywhere. Laura dealt with each customer without interruption, even when she was being asked questions. Her insides were hard as nails. She was determined to maintain control. Her body was weak from hunger since she had not had a chance to stop and eat. Filled with fatigue, her legs could barely support her, yet she continued on. She had given up on George Fitzgerald. Her only hope now was that everyone would finish shopping and leave and no one else would come in.

"What's the matter, dear?" asked a matronly store patron.

"I am just so tired," Laura replied.

Eight o'clock. Laura thought of closing the store at eight thirty. Yes, that's what she would do. What would Fitzgerald do... fire her? It did not seem to matter now. All she could think about was her children and their disappointment on Christmas morning. No presents! No Santa Claus! Tears welled up in her eyes.

The customers were thinning out. Only a few shoppers were left. It was eight fifteen. Sullivan's Toy Shop would close at nine. Laura quickly placed the "Closed" sign in the window. She asked those customers remaining to complete their shopping since the store was closing. This did not seem to bother anyone.

Easy as one, two, three, she thought.

Eight thirty. Laura was ringing up the purchases of her last shopper. She began to feel calm. Three minutes later, she locked the door. The store was empty now, except for Laura.

I just need to ring out the register, empty the till, and count the money, she thought.

Laura worked quickly. She put the money in the safe that Mr. Fitzgerald had in his office and retrieved her coat, hat, and mittens. "It is 8:41... no problem. I need to hurry to get to Sullivan's," she told herself quietly. Lights out. Store closed!

Laura had been so busy that she had not noticed the snow falling outside. A small storm had settled in, and it was quite windy.

It normally took her ten minutes walking briskly in good weather to get to the toy shop. Laura had no money to spare for a cab fare, even if she could have hailed a cab in what was fast becoming a real blizzard.

No wonder the store had emptied so quickly, she thought.

Laura trudged through the snow as fast as her exhausted legs could move. The wind was against her, and it was difficult to see. She knew where she was going, and nothing could stop her. She was determined to get to Sullivan's before it closed. She looked down at her watch... 8:50. She felt total despair! Her body ached with pain and her heart ready to burst! Laura Winchester, sales clerk, cleaning woman, and mother, had worked so hard, and she was so close to Sullivan's. Time was running out!

Laura thought of her children and how happy they would be on Christmas morning. She could see their smiling faces. Her body was totally spent, but her will was stronger. The toy store was within sight. She glanced at her watch... 8:56. Almost there. She mustered every fiber in her body. She began to run against the blinding snow and wind. She was at Sullivan's door... 8:58. She had made it! Her hand quickly encircled the door's knob, but it would not turn. The door would not open. She pounded on the door. Fear entered her mind. Her heart was almost broken. Her eyes were full of tears.

At that moment, Laura noticed the sign in the shop's window: "Closed."

"It can't be! It just can't be!" she sobbed, and tears flowed down her cheeks.

Laura pounded on the door again with faint hope that some-one was still there. No one came. No one heard her knocks. It was dark inside. She noticed the clock on the wall inside... 8:59. She looked down at her watch... 8:59. Then she noticed a second sign in Sullivan's window: "This store will close at 8:00 p.m. on December 23. We will reopen for business at 10:00 a.m. on December 26. Merry Christmas."

Totally defeated, Laura looked to the heavens and cried, "Why, God, why?"

Laura's heart was breaking. Her legs gave way, and she crumbled to the ground. She sobbed openly. Her children's Christmas presents were locked inside Sullivan's. Even if she had more money, all the stores were closed. Minutes passed. Laura was too tired to stand up. Her sobs continued. The streets were empty, except for buses and a few cars that were exiting Boston's business district. No one noticed Laura lying on the ground. The snow quickly formed a white blanket over her. Her sobbing went unnoticed, heard only to the wind.

The blizzard and the wind began to ease up. Laura brushed the snow off her tired, aching body and slowly rose to her feet. She eventually made her way back to Fitzgerald's. It was 9:40 when she opened the door of the store. Only an hour before, this had been her prison. The customers had been her enemies.

Laura slowly looked over the depleted shelves where George Fitzgerald stocked inexpensive toys and games. There was nothing left that was even remotely suitable for her children. There was nothing she could do. Laura sunk to her knees and began to sob uncontrollably. At that moment, the door opened and a very drunk Fitzgerald stumbled in.

"Was worried I'd mished ya," he slurred. "Here's yer bonus."

As Laura reached out for the envelope that was wadded up in Fitzgerald's hand, he collapsed to the floor. She watched in disbelief as he began to snore.

Inside the envelope was a check for five dollars.

"Too little! Too late!" she exclaimed.

With total disdain, she tore up the check and threw the pieces at the sleeping Fitzgerald—a poor excuse of a man!

As Laura washed and waxed the floors at Bonnie Pratt's that evening, she vowed, "Next week, I will find a new job. Yes, that is what I will do!" She knew full well she would not.

Sunday, December 24, 1950

Morning worship services were at nine o'clock. Sara and Sam were dressed in their Sunday best. Although tired and weather beaten, Laura looked beautiful in her new dress. It was not the expensive suit that she had admired at Bonnie Pratt's. It was not even a store-bought dress. She had made the dress herself.

Laura held her head up high as she entered the church. There would be no stares. She did not need them. She was a proud woman. Laura was there with her children to worship the Lord. Tomorrow, the world would celebrate his birthday. Tomorrow, Laura's world would fall apart.

Following the service, Laura, Sara, and Sam sang Christmas carols inside their Plymouth as they made their way to St. Albans, accompanied by gently falling snow.

Laura

My heart is heavy.
Often I am sad.
For once we were four,
Now we are three.
Our years were so few.
It seems so unfair,
Yet, the years will multiply
Our family tree.

I work so hard.
The hours are long.
The pay is so little,
My pennies are few.
I go two steps forward,
Then, fall back three.
The burden is heavy,
Life is not free.

My best friend is gone.
Despair, my constant companion.
I find it so hard.
My smiles are so few.
My children are my life,
For them, I must press on.
I daydream a lot.
It's all I can do.

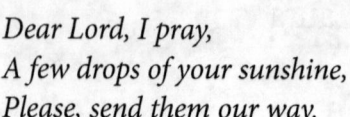

Dear Lord, I pray,
A few drops of your sunshine,
Please, send them our way.

Journal entry of Laura Winchester
October 10, 1946

Laura, Sam & Sara

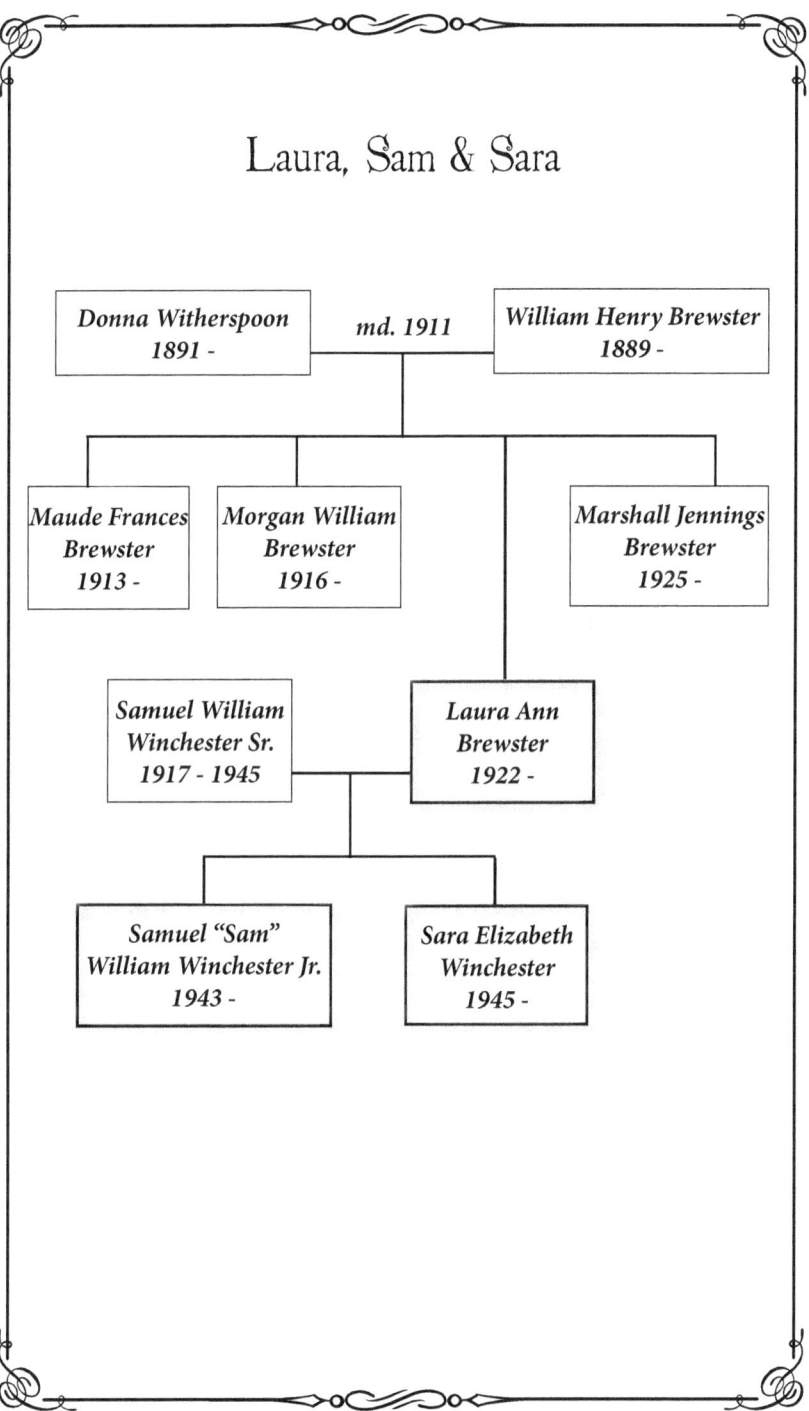

| Donna Witherspoon 1891 - | md. 1911 | William Henry Brewster 1889 - |

- Maude Frances Brewster 1913 -
- Morgan William Brewster 1916 -
- Marshall Jennings Brewster 1925 -

- Samuel William Winchester Sr. 1917 - 1945
- Laura Ann Brewster 1922 -

- Samuel "Sam" William Winchester Jr. 1943 -
- Sara Elizabeth Winchester 1945 -

Chapter Two

――○◦⌒◦○――

Maverick

George Washington Maverick Jr. was born in 1866 on his father's ranch in Shackelford County, Texas, about fifteen miles northeast of Abilene. When he was fourteen years old, his parents sent him east in hopes of his gaining a good education. He went to live with his maternal grandparents in Middleton, New York. However, he gained a different kind of education than the one his parents expected. He learned to play baseball, and he learned to play it well. Along the way, he acquired the nickname: Dutch.

Dutch played professional baseball for Boston in the National League. Boston's team was known as the Red Stockings when he began his career with them in 1884. By the time his playing days were over, in 1895, they were more commonly called the Boston Beaneaters. Later they would be known as the Braves. For a brief time, from 1936 through April 1941, they were known as the "Bees".

A scrappy second baseman, Dutch had a career batting average of .301. He continued with the team as a coach until

May 1898. At that time, he returned to Texas and joined Teddy Roosevelt's Rough Riders, who were being trained at Fort Sam Houston in San Antonio. Dutch fought as a Rough Rider during the brief Spanish-American War.

Following the war, Dutch teamed up with several of his war buddies and joined the Klondike gold rush in the Canadian Yukon. This was followed by a mining venture in South America. In 1903, after an absence of twenty-three years, he returned to the family ranch in Texas. He was thirty-seven years old and still single. In Dutch's mind, he was an old man facing his final days of what many of his friends referred to as a "remarkable life."

In baseball Dutch was known for not letting his team down. He seemed to thrive under pressure. When the Red Stockings needed a hit to win the game, he got a hit. Playing defense, he was known for stopping a sure single and turning what often appeared as a game winner into the front end of a game-ending double play. With any game on the line, Dutch's teammates were confident of the outcome when the bat or ball was in Dutch's hands.

Whether as a ball player, soldier, or miner, Dutch Maverick was always successful. What appeared in 1903 to be the final years of his life were not, in fact the best days of his life were still to come.

Ranching was the least of Dutch's priorities. Fortunately for the Maverick family, George Washington Maverick Sr. lived to be 101 and managed the ranch's operation until the end of his life. He enjoyed perfect health until he passed away in his sleep in 1942.

On September 3, 1913, Dutch married Serelda Case of Abilene, Texas. Dutch was forty-seven, and she was twenty-three. Dutch and Serelda had six children, five daughters and one son: Margaret, Mary Ellen, Martha, Constance, Barbara Ann, and Jonathan Case Maverick. Dutch wanted a son to whom he could teach baseball. George Sr. wanted a grandson to whom he could teach ranching. George Sr. had to settle with his granddaughter, Mary Ellen. In the years to follow, she would devote all her time to ranching.

The day Dutch's only son, Johnny Maverick, was born in 1920, Dutch placed a baseball in Johnny's crib so he would become familiar with it. Before he could walk, Johnny was taught how to throw the ball. He was taught how to hit the ball before he could run. Dutch managed a semipro baseball team in Abilene from 1904 through 1939. In his early years, Johnny was the team's mascot, then their bat boy, and by age twelve, he became their center fielder. At that time, he was five feet eight inches tall and weighed 150 pounds. By his sixteenth birthday, he had become six feet tall and weighed a solid 190. Johnny had speed in the outfield and on the bases. He was a power hitter who could also hit for average. He was considered a top professional prospect.

Johnny's natural talent and years of playing semipro baseball helped mature his game well beyond his years. In 1937, at age seventeen, he signed a professional contract to play for the Boston Bees. He would be playing for the same team for which his father both played and coached. This was a dream come true not only for Johnny but also for Dutch.

George Sr. loved and admired his only grandson. For most of his 101 years, Grandpa Maverick felt that baseball was for foolish and idle people. By the time he passed away, he had become pretty proud not only of his grandson's ability to play but also of Dutch's baseball career.

Following high school graduation in 1937, Johnny was asked to join the team at home in Boston for a few days. After that, he was supposed to be assigned to one of the team's minor league affiliates. However, after a strong display of power during several batting practice sessions, Johnny was given the opportunity to remain with the team when a player became injured for the season. Johnny was informed that this would be only a temporary stay with the mother club. He would be used only as a pinch hitter and pinch runner.

For the next few weeks, Johnny was not given any opportunity to play. He spent his bench time well, studying the players and how they played on the major league level. Late in June, the Bees were playing the Cardinals at home. It was the bottom of the ninth inning, and Boston was losing 4–2. With two outs and runners on first and second, the pitcher was up, and the Bees were down to their last out. Johnny was announced as the pinch hitter. In total control of his nerves and confident of his ability, he took his place in the batter's box. The crowd was on their feet and the noise level was deafening. Johnny, was in the zone and didn't hear the crowd. His focus was on looking for just the right pitch. The first two pitches were called strikes, but Johnny passed on both, as neither was to his liking. The next two were called balls. Then, he got the pitch he was looking for and drove the ball over the wall in the deepest part of center field. The Bees won the game, and a new hero was born.

As a part-time player in 1937, Johnny had ten home runs and thirty-seven runs batted in, and he batted a solid .283. By 1941, Johnny had become one of the league's most valuable players. He blasted twenty-nine home runs, knocked in 113 runs, and batted .319. He was second in the league in all of these statistical categories. In May 1941, the Bees became known once again as the Braves.

Boston was excited about Johnny Maverick. He had made it to the major leagues without ever playing in a minor league game. He was fast becoming one of the stars of the National League. After five seasons in the majors, at only twenty-one years of age, Johnny was headed for a Hall of Fame career. He had matured early but was far from reaching his prime.

Instead of reporting to the Braves and hitting home runs in 1942, Johnny was at Camp Hood in Texas, being trained as a tank destroyer. He wanted to serve his country, so he had enlisted in the army the day after the attack on Pearl Harbor. His battalion was sent to North Africa in early 1943, and he was promoted to the rank of corporal.

Johnny fought against Rommel's German forces in North Africa. After D-day, he fought through Sicily and up through Italy. Shortly after he was promoted to sergeant, he was seriously injured in southern Italy and evacuated to a military hospital in England. There he fell deeply in love with Mary Alice Hope, an English nurse.

Though Johnny's injuries were severe, his spirits were high. He and Mary Alice planned to marry as soon as he could walk down the aisle on his own. "I won't have you marrying an invalid!" he told her. Their happiness and his recovery were short-lived when Mary Alice was killed in an ambulance crash.

Sergeant Johnny Maverick went into deep depression. He was evacuated to the United States for convalescence at Brooke General Hospital at Fort Sam Houston in Texas. His depression lingered. The severity of the injuries to his arms and legs meant his career as a baseball player was over. He would walk with a limp the remainder of his life, but the damage to his spirit was what most concerned his doctors. It was the winter of 1945, and the war continued.

***

Mary Catherine Seymour, fondly known as Molly, was born in Winooski, Vermont. She was the daughter of Dr. Franklin Samuel Seymour and Rachel Adams. Rachel never knew her parents. Her mother, Catherine, died of complications during Rachel's birth. She was only sixteen and unmarried. Catherine's widowed mother, Sabrina Fowler, took the infant into her home, planning to raise her. Unfortunately, she unexpectedly died of pneumonia the following year. The infant was quickly welcomed into the home of a close relative, Aunt Patty, and her husband, Dr. Samuel Adams. They were an older couple and had been childless. They showered a lot of love and attention on Rachel and raised her as their own.

Rachel was trained as a nurse and worked with Dr. Adams and his young protégé, Dr. Franklin S. Seymour. She and Dr. Seymour were married in 1910. Their son, Samuel, was born in 1914, and Molly followed in 1922. Tragically, Rachel died when Molly was only one.

Molly's older brother, Samuel, completed medical school at John Hopkins University in the spring of 1942. He was commissioned in the army and took his residency at Brooke General Hospital at Fort Sam Houston in San Antonio, Texas. His wife and two young daughters accompanied him. Two additional daughters and two sons eventually blessed their home.

After high school graduation in 1939, Molly enrolled at Boston College. Upon graduation in 1943, she returned to Winooski to work in the office of the family medical clinic. From the time Molly turned three to the time she went to college, Dr. Seymour believed that he might be raising the first woman baseball or football player. She would outhit or outslide any neighborhood boy her age, and she fell asleep at night with a football in her arms. She had her share of bloody noses and broken bones. She often came home sporting a black eye. Dr. Seymour would ask Molly, "Who won?" Molly would always reply, bragging, "I did! You ought to see the two shiners and bloody nose I gave him!"

As a child and teenager, Molly wore her hair short and dirty. The pretty young lady who returned to Winooski in 1943 was in sharp contrast to the adolescent without makeup four years earlier. The difference was night and day. Molly turned in her blue jeans with knee patches for laced blouses and full skirts. Long, flowing hair, makeup, and a purse replaced the tomboy that Dr. Seymour was sure he raised. Always sure of herself, Molly was a perfect picture of someone who knew exactly where she was headed.

In the winter of 1945, Molly received an invitation from Samuel and his wife to visit them for Easter. This would be her first visit to Texas. Molly had not seen her brother and his family for nearly three years. She eagerly accepted the invitation.

Samuel was not able to meet Molly's train when it arrived in San Antonio. His wife, Sylvia, was there to welcome Molly. After collecting Molly's bags, Sylvia and Molly drove to Fort Sam Houston to pick up Samuel. They had an hour to spare before he was free to leave.

Sylvia took Molly on a quick tour of the army hospital and its grounds. It was the day before Good Friday and a pleasant spring day. Molly noticed a young man sitting in a wheelchair under the shade of an oak tree. He was staring at the ground, with his head drooped, and he looked extremely sad and forlorn. He was very pale and thin. His cheeks were sallow, and he looked as though he had not eaten in months.

"He looks very sad, doesn't he?" commented Molly. She could not take her eyes off the young soldier.

Sylvia replied, "Do you have any idea who that soldier is?"

Molly studied the soldier's face. "I don't recognize him. Is he someone I should know?"

"That is Johnny Maverick. He was the star center fielder for the Boston Braves before the war. Many felt that he would be the next Lou Gehrig." Sylvia continued to note his many exploits on the baseball diamond, but Molly's thoughts drowned out Sylvia's comments.

Molly remembered Johnny Maverick. As a fan of the Boston Braves, she had watched him play many times. The Johnny Maverick that she remembered was extremely handsome, tall, and muscular. He had an air of confidence about him, which impressed everyone who watched him play. He was focused on his craft. He not only was a great athlete but was also known as one of those rare individuals who gave more to the game, to his community, and to his fans than he took. It was hard for Molly to comprehend that the Johnny Maverick she had once idolized had been reduced so greatly in body and spirit in the space of just a few years.

Molly walked slowly toward Johnny. She sat down on the grass in front of him and looked up into his eyes. "Mind if I sit here?" she questioned.

There was no reply.

Molly looked deeply into Johnny's eyes. As he returned the gaze, she recognized something very special. Never in her life had she seen eyes that seemed so warm and so gentle. A wonderful feeling rushed through her. She felt complete peace and compassion deep within herself for this soldier. Molly saw him in a totally different light.

A smile appeared on Johnny's face. Was he staring at an angel? Had he died and gone to heaven? He knew he was still on earth, but he felt that in that very moment, the Lord was sharing a part of heaven with him. As he continued to stare into Molly's eyes, he felt her warmth and her love, and a familiar sensation went through his body. He recognized this feeling. He had known it well with his precious Mary Alice—his kind, gentle, loving Mary Alice, who was so tragically taken from him.

Johnny reached out with his right hand and carefully touched Molly's cheek. Tears began to flow from her eyes. Molly gently placed Johnny's left hand to her lips as he tenderly stroked her face and her hair with the fingers of his right hand. This is not a dream. *She is here, familiar but different.*

"Well, I'll be!" exclaimed a shocked Dr. Samuel Seymour as he joined Sylvia in witnessing this miracle. "Nobody has been able to reach him—at least, not until now."

Molly extended her visit and spent nearly all her time with Johnny at the hospital. With Molly's love and encouragement, Johnny's recovery progressed rapidly. Molly was all the therapy

Johnny needed.

After a brief courtship, Johnny and Molly were married on September 22, 1945. They moved to the family ranch, where Johnny worked during the next year as he continued to rebuild his body.

In the fall of 1946, he enrolled as a student at the University of Texas at Austin. Johnny was grateful that his mother had urged him to attend college during the off-seasons while he was playing professional baseball. He was only two years shy of completing his degree in education.

Johnny graduated in the spring of 1948 and received his master's degree in educational administration two years later. While working on his master's, he became an assistant baseball coach at the university.

Johnny was still quite popular in New England and received offers for several teaching positions. The one that most appealed to him was at a high school in Montpelier, Vermont, coaching baseball and football and teaching civics and history. This also appealed to Molly, since Montpelier was only forty miles from her family in Winooski.

Christmas 1950 would be extra special for Johnny and Molly. After two miscarriages, they were expecting their first child. The baby was due December 29. Molly wanted to spend Christmas with her family in Winooski. She and Johnny had spent their first five Christmases with his family in Texas, and she was looking forward to an old-fashioned Christmas with her family in Vermont. She wanted to deliver her child in surroundings that were familiar to her. Johnny reluctantly went along with his wife's wishes.

Following worship services on Christmas Eve, Johnny and Molly enjoyed a brunch with friends. It was a peaceful Sunday afternoon. Their car was packed and ready for the drive to Winooski.

As Johnny and Molly exited the city of Montpelier, Johnny

noted that the time was 4:20 p.m. The sun had set only min-utes before. With good weather, they should make the trip in an hour. Johnny was not in a hurry today. The Seymour family was not expecting them until six o'clock or shortly thereafter. *Plenty of time,* thought Johnny, not paying much attention to the snowflakes that were beginning to fall.

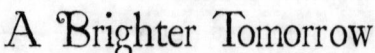

A Brighter Tomorrow

No one can foresee the challenges
    And opportunities that lie ahead in their life.
No one can know what is around
    The next corner, and how it will affect them.

Sometimes, what seems to be the greatest tragedy
    Is but the closing of one door, and the opening of another,
Into a greater field of opportunity, or experience,
    To be unmatched by no other.

Sometimes, we lose a loved one,
    And we think our life is over.
Sometimes, we feel our burdens
    Are more than we can bear.

Time has a way of healing,
    And we must remember that
Our Father in Heaven is always there for us,
    And He will hear our prayers and answer them.

We must be willing to be patient, listen,
    And open up our minds and our hearts.
Ofttimes, the answers our Father gives to us
    Are not the ones we wish to hear.

In the autumn of our life,
And as we are reflecting back,
Perhaps, we will finally realize the purpose of our life:
That there always is a better and brighter tomorrow!

Journal entry of Johnny Maverick
August 19, 1996

Johnny

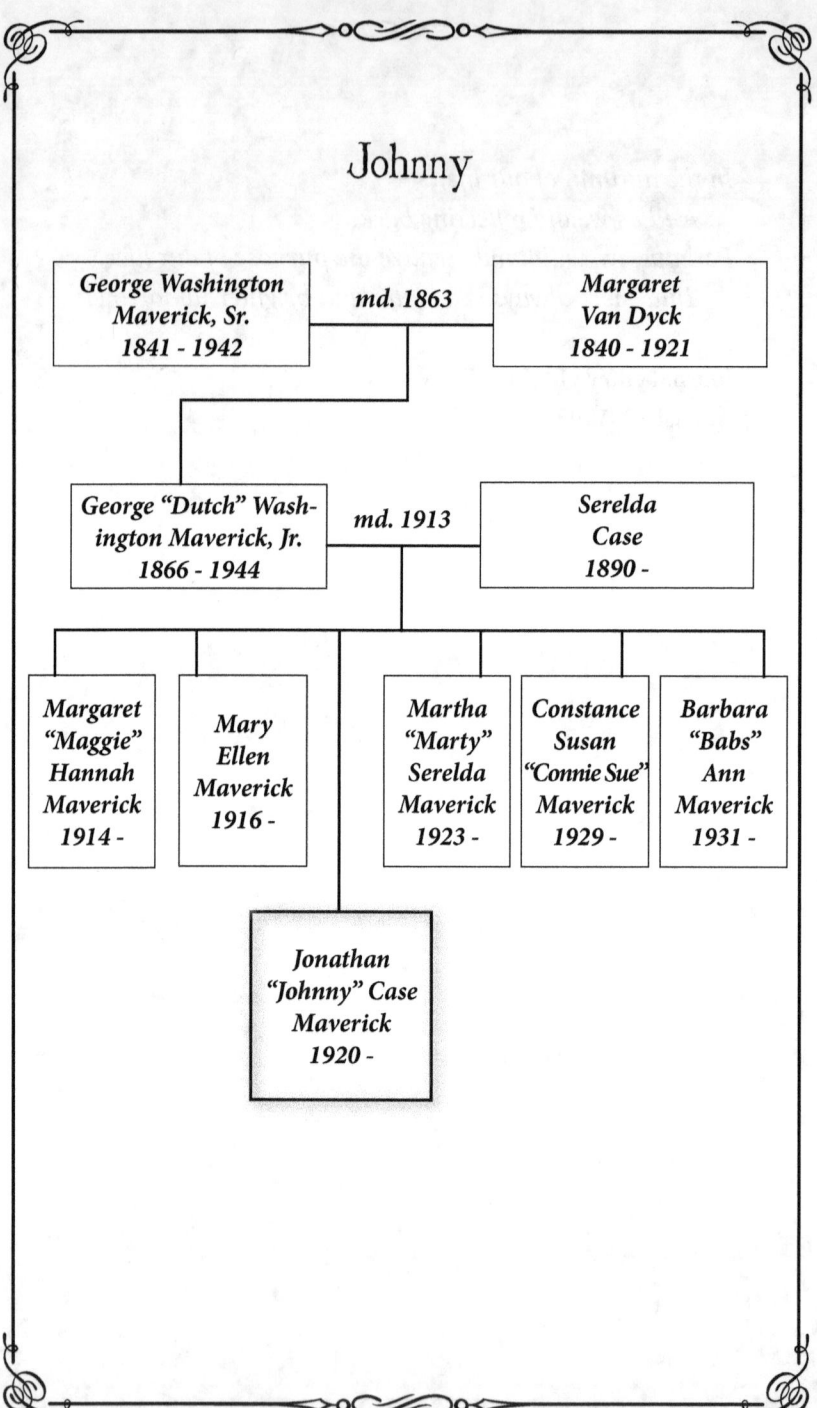

George Washington Maverick, Sr. 1841 - 1942 — **md. 1863** — Margaret Van Dyck 1840 - 1921

George "Dutch" Washington Maverick, Jr. 1866 - 1944 — **md. 1913** — Serelda Case 1890 -

Margaret "Maggie" Hannah Maverick 1914 -

Mary Ellen Maverick 1916 -

Martha "Marty" Serelda Maverick 1923 -

Constance Susan "Connie Sue" Maverick 1929 -

Barbara "Babs" Ann Maverick 1931 -

Jonathan "Johnny" Case Maverick 1920 -

Molly

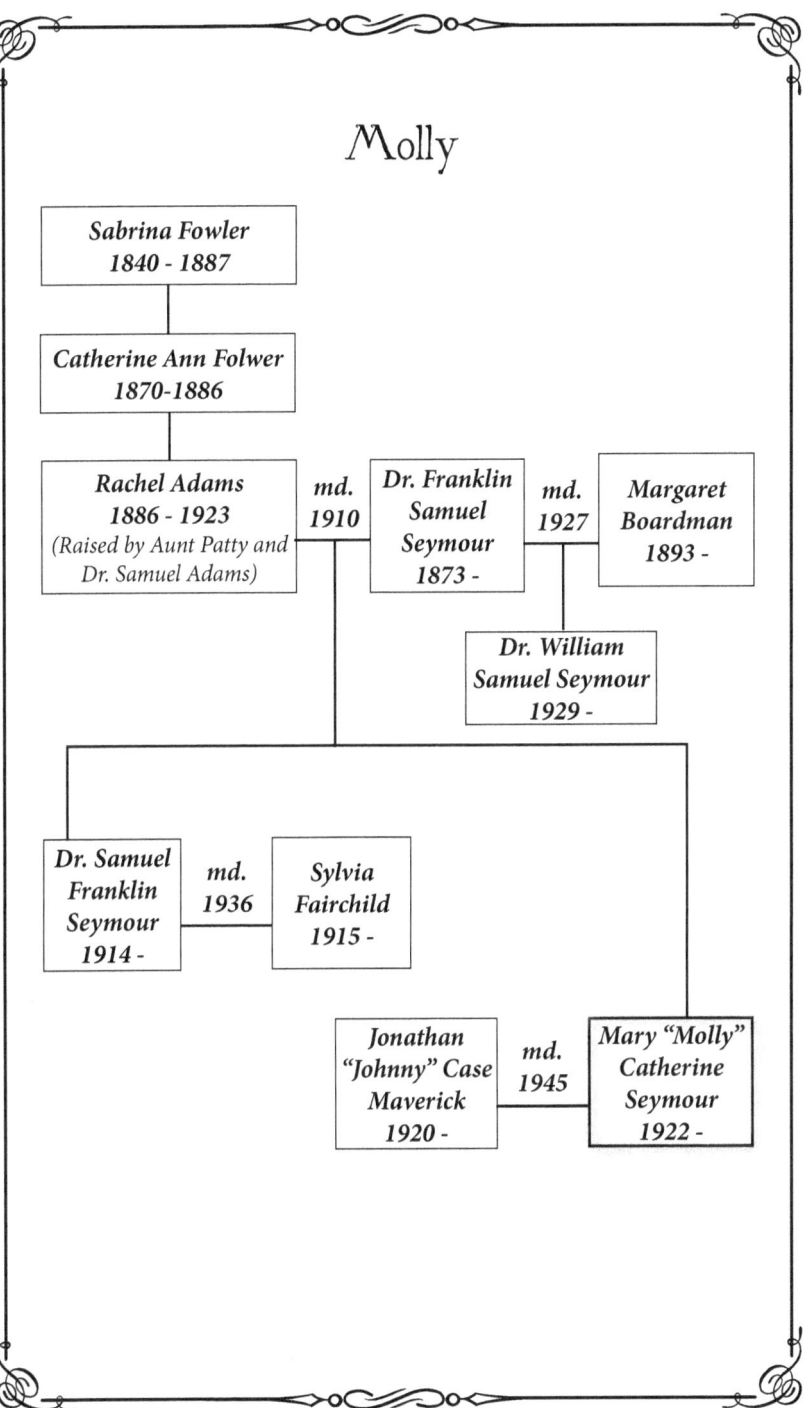

Sabrina Fowler
1840 - 1887

Catherine Ann Folwer
1870-1886

Rachel Adams
1886 - 1923
*(Raised by Aunt Patty and
Dr. Samuel Adams)*

md.
1910

Dr. Franklin
Samuel
Seymour
1873 -

md.
1927

Margaret
Boardman
1893 -

Dr. William
Samuel Seymour
1929 -

Dr. Samuel
Franklin
Seymour
1914 -

md.
1936

Sylvia
Fairchild
1915 -

Jonathan
"Johnny" Case
Maverick
1920 -

md.
1945

Mary "Molly"
Catherine
Seymour
1922 -

Chapter Three

Masters

Frank Masters lived to work. He enjoyed his position as president of Niagara Tool and Die Company of Lowell, Massachusetts. He started as a sales representative shortly after returning from France, where he served during World War I.

Frank was born in Lowell in 1898, the eldest of eight children. His parents, Stephen and Alice Masters, emigrated from Liverpool, England, soon after their marriage in 1897.

Stephen's older brother, Charles, had immigrated to America six years earlier, in 1891, and found employment as a machinist for Niagara Tool and Die Company. He used his savings to bring Stephen and Alice to America.

Stephen went to work at Niagara, as did his brother-in-law, Harry Miller, when Harry arrived in 1903. The families remained a close-knit group for years, but Frank was the only second-generation family member to stay with the company.

By 1950, Frank was the only member of his immediate family still living in Lowell. With the exception of several cousins, the remainder of the Masters and Miller descendants had moved west and scattered throughout the United States.

In the early years of his employment, Frank's sales area covered part of the state of Maine. He would leave Lowell before dawn on Monday and return after dark on Friday. He became one of the top sales producers for Niagara. In 1926, he was promoted to district sales manager. He moved to Concord, New Hampshire, where the district office was located. Niagara was one of the largest tool and die companies in America. Frank's district covered all of Maine, New Hampshire, and Vermont.

In the spring of 1927, one of Frank's salesmen, Alfred Pratt, introduced Frank to his sister Martha. She was only eighteen, eleven years younger than Frank. On Frank and Martha's second date, Frank asked Martha to be his wife. Martha's widowed mother, Anne, liked Frank and approved of the match. Frank and Martha were married in Mrs. Pratt's home in Concord on June 1, 1927, two weeks to the day after their first date. Alfred was Frank's best man. Martha's uncle, Walker Pratt, gave her away, and Martha's sister, Margaret, was her maid of honor. Frank and Martha exuded happiness and delighted in their newfound love

For Anne Marie Fowler Pratt, Martha's wedding was an answer to prayer. Anne was forty-three years old when she delivered Martha, her eighth child. Anne's husband, Alfred Pratt Sr., had passed away with pneumonia two months before Martha was born. The years had taken their toll on Anne, who was left with seven other children to raise, ranging in age from three to twenty-three.

Alfred Pratt Sr. had been a watchmaker. His family owned Pratt Watch Company in Concord. Though not a large company, the inheritance Alfred Sr.'s father left him was sufficient to provide a comfortable living for Anne and her children. Although Pratt Watch Company no longer existed, Anne still had enough to provide for her modest lifestyle.

Anne was totally dedicated to her children and their happiness. All of her children were happily married, and at age sixty-one, Anne felt that her life was complete. Within a year, she also succumb to pneumonia and join her beloved Alfred.

Anne had never known her natural parents, nor did she ever learn what happened to them. She was raised by her mother's sister Sabrina but was never formally adopted. When Anne was eighteen, she learned that Sabrina was not her natural mother. Sabrina's husband, Michael Fowler, died when Anne was fourteen. Four years later, Michael's mother, Anne Barlow Fowler, passed away. As she left no will, her sole heirs were Michael's children and Michael's brother, John. The heirs were listed in the petition of administration as follows: "Children of son Michael Fowler Sr., deceased: Michael Jr., age seventeen; Catherine, age fourteen; Mary, age eleven; Ethan, age seven; and Rev. John Fowler, son, age thirty-six."

Anne was not listed. She did not know why. Neither did her siblings. It was at this time that Sabrina broke down and told Anne that she and Michael were not her natural parents. Anne was the illegitimate daughter of Sabrina's sister. However, Sabrina and Michael loved Anne as though she were their own. Sabrina and Michael chose to be her parents because they wanted her, and that made her even more special to them.

In 1866, Sabrina and Michael had been married about two years and had no children. Even though they lived in another town, they were present when Anne was born. They arranged with Sabrina's sister to take Anne and raise her as their own. She would never be told about her origin. Her natural mother would go away and start a new life.

When Anne was ten days old, Sabrina and Michael also left and moved to Concord, New Hampshire. Sabrina never heard from her sister again. Although Sabrina knew who Anne's father was, she had promised to never reveal his identity. It was a promise that Sabrina honored to her dying breath.

Uncle John Fowler was the administrator of his mother's estate. Being a minister and extremely pious, he felt he could not further "the great lie." He had never approved of Michael raising "that illegitimate child," as he referred to Anne. He was never warm to her. Now Anne realized why. Anne Barlow Fowler treated her as one of her own grandchildren, and Anne had always felt as though she was the favorite. This made the hurt and inner grief more intense.

Uncle John petitioned the court and was appointed guardian of his nieces and nephews. This put him in control of their inheritance from their grandmother's estate. He always made it a point to portion out the inheritance in front of Anne, as a constant reminder of her illegitimate birth.

Although Anne's younger siblings considered her as one of them, and even though Anne was given an equal share in Sabrina's will, she never felt the same again. She wondered who she really was and why she should have to suffer for her natural parents' transgression. She had been given lots of love from the day of her birth. Only Uncle John made her feel lesser. She vowed, that none of her children would ever suffer as she had.

***

Frank's new position with Niagara Tool and Die Company, in 1927 required some travel, but he was home 75 percent of the time, working in the district office in Concord. Each time Frank was away, Martha missed him immensely. When he returned, his passion toward her intensified. When she became pregnant, he was even more attentive to her needs. She felt his protective love constantly.

Shirley Anne Masters entered the world on the first day of spring, March 21, 1928. Frank's behavior toward Martha changed soon after. When Shirley Anne was born, Frank waited on Martha night and day. He also managed to remain in Concord, without any business travel, until Shirley Anne was three months old. Frank appeared to be a devoted father and husband, but Martha sensed some turmoil going on inside him. She hoped this change was only due to pressure at work.

Martha did not want to ask him why he had changed. It occurred to her that she had never heard Frank tell her that he loved her since she had known him. However, she knew he loved her deeply. She sensed it was just something he could not say, even though he felt it.

Frank was somewhat affectionate, but Frank and Martha's love life was not what it had been in the past. Sometimes, Frank would give Martha a hug and a brief kiss; other times, he would reach out and hold her hand. In the privacy of their bed, he held his wife in his arms and kissed her cheek or forehead, nothing more.

Frank seemed to become more distant with each passing day. He had always been quiet but seemed to talk to Martha less and less. Martha began to resent her husband's near-total withdrawal. Evenings would pass with Frank hardly saying a word.

Just as Martha began to accept her plight, Frank startled her one night by declaring his love for her. He held her in his arms and whispered, "You and Shirley Anne mean the world to me. I love you both so much. I can't imagine life without you." Tears of joy rolled down Martha's cheeks, and Martha fell asleep in his arms. Although things did not progress any further, Martha felt she and Frank were becoming closer, and she was more content than she had been in months.

Several days later, when Frank came home from work, Martha sensed something different about him. He was brimming with excitement. He swept up Martha in his arms and carried her into their bedroom.

"You will never guess what happened!" he exclaimed. "You're looking at the new manager of the Eastern States region. That means we're moving to the corporate home office in my hometown of Lowell, Massachusetts!"

Frank leaned back on the bed and pulled Martha next to him. From that moment on, Frank no longer held back from expressing his affection for his beloved wife. Life was finally back to normal in the Masters household.

Frank later confided to Martha that a few months before Shirley Anne was born, he learned that his regional manager would be retiring at the end of the year. This was the position Frank had worked so hard to attain. However, he had been afraid that it would be given to David Maguire, son of the vice president of marketing. Maguire had been with Niagara only a few years. Although there were others more deserving, David Maguire was made a district manager just eighteen months after he started. Frank seriously thought that he would be passed over in favor of Maguire.

Frank never apologized to Martha for his distant behavior. Nor did she ever tell him of the agony she had suffered. He seldom told Martha he loved her, but that did not matter. Martha knew her husband loved her, and she was content.

On April 15, 1930, twin babies, Franklin Marion Masters Jr. and Frances Anne Masters were born fourteen weeks premature. Franklin died the next day, and Frances followed him two days later. Both were born with defective hearts, and their lungs had not fully developed. Frank and Martha never recovered from the loss of their babies. They were devastated and unable able to share their grief, which caused them to withdraw from each other.

Frank focused more on his career, oftentimes bringing home a full briefcase and working late into the night. Martha joined several garden and women's clubs. Frank and Martha's love for Shirley Anne became the only thing that held them together.

In 1935, Frank was promoted to assistant vice president of marketing. Three years later, he became the vice president of marketing and was appointed to the board of directors. Niagara Tool and Die Company was becoming one of the leading corporations in America. Frank and Martha were members of the Lowell Country Club and lived in one of the more affluent sections of the city. Martha became president of the garden club. In 1945, at age forty-seven, Frank was named president of Niagara Tool and Die Company. Socially, professionally, and financially, he had made it to the very top of the ladder.

In 1944, at age sixteen, Shirley Anne graduated from a private high school, Lowell Female Academy. She attended Brown University and graduated with honors in 1948. In June of that year, she became the bride of Dr. Sterling William Cook Jr. They moved to Burlington, Vermont, where he became a partner in his father's medical practice. Their first child, Martha Anne, was born the following July.

Frank and Martha Masters now found themselves all alone— so alone!

On Christmas Eve 1950, their spirits were high because they were going to spend Christmas in Burlington with Shirley Anne and her family.

Our Babies

Our hearts were full,
  When we learned one day,
Two spirits were coming,
  To our home to stay.

A twist of fate, perhaps,
  The doctors said that day.
They were born too early,
  Would be unable to stay.

Our hearts were broken.
  Our loss, so sad!
Our babies were taken.
  From their mom and dad.

The cemetery is cold,
  Where our children lay.
We visit them often.
  Tears flow their way.

There is no solace.
  There is no peace.
Our house is empty
  Of little feet.

Why were our babies
  Taken from us that day?
Was it something we did?
  Such a terrible price to pay!

Do our children continue
  To grow and be old?
Or, do their lives end,
  When they are dead and cold?

We look to the heavens,
  As we say our prayers.
Please, give us the answer,
  To the burden we bear.

Journal entry of Martha Masters
January 24, 1931

The Fowler Family

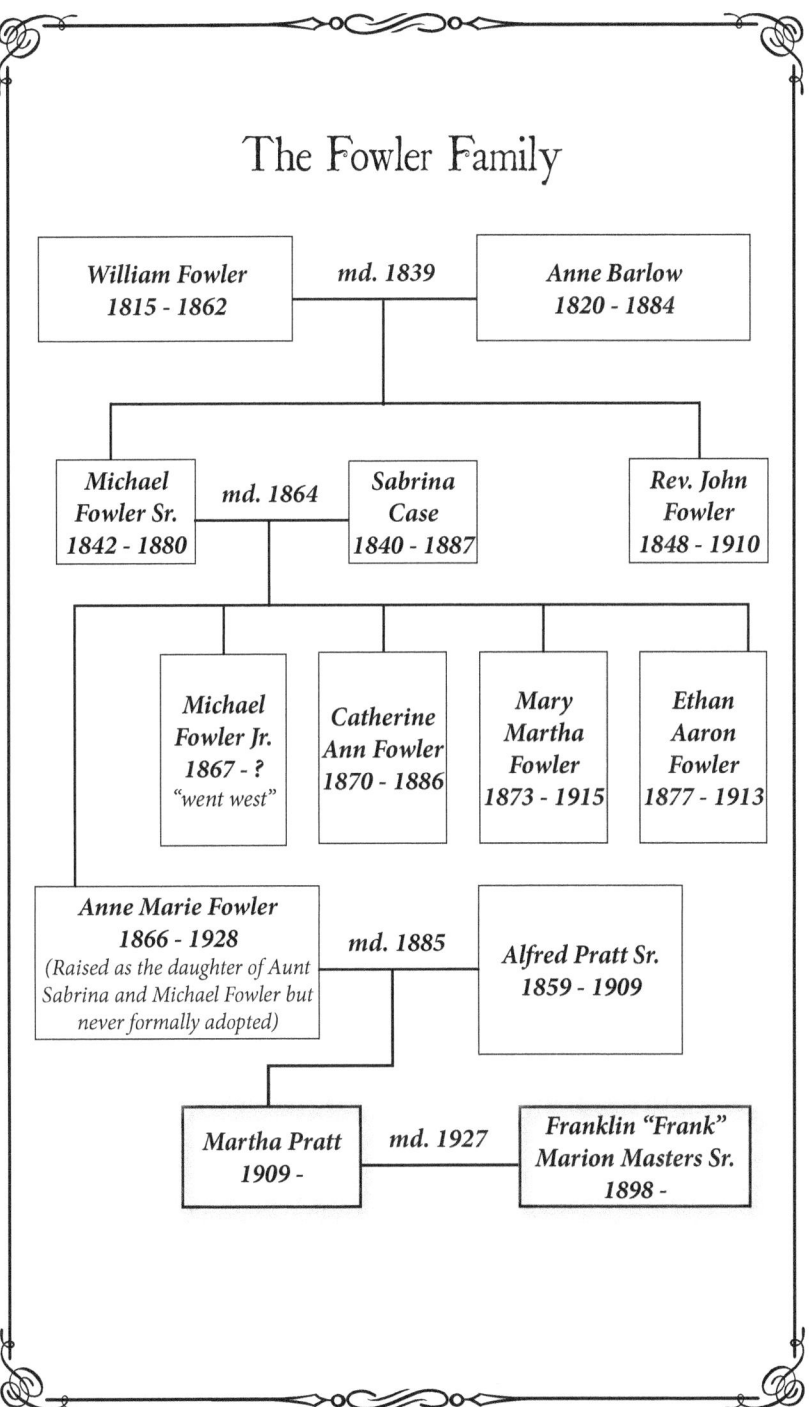

William Fowler
1815 - 1862

md. 1839

Anne Barlow
1820 - 1884

Michael
Fowler Sr.
1842 - 1880

md. 1864

Sabrina
Case
1840 - 1887

Rev. John
Fowler
1848 - 1910

Michael
Fowler Jr.
1867 - ?
"went west"

Catherine
Ann Fowler
1870 - 1886

Mary
Martha
Fowler
1873 - 1915

Ethan
Aaron
Fowler
1877 - 1913

Anne Marie Fowler
1866 - 1928
(Raised as the daughter of Aunt
Sabrina and Michael Fowler but
never formally adopted)

md. 1885

Alfred Pratt Sr.
1859 - 1909

Martha Pratt
1909 -

md. 1927

Franklin "Frank"
Marion Masters Sr.
1898 -

Martha

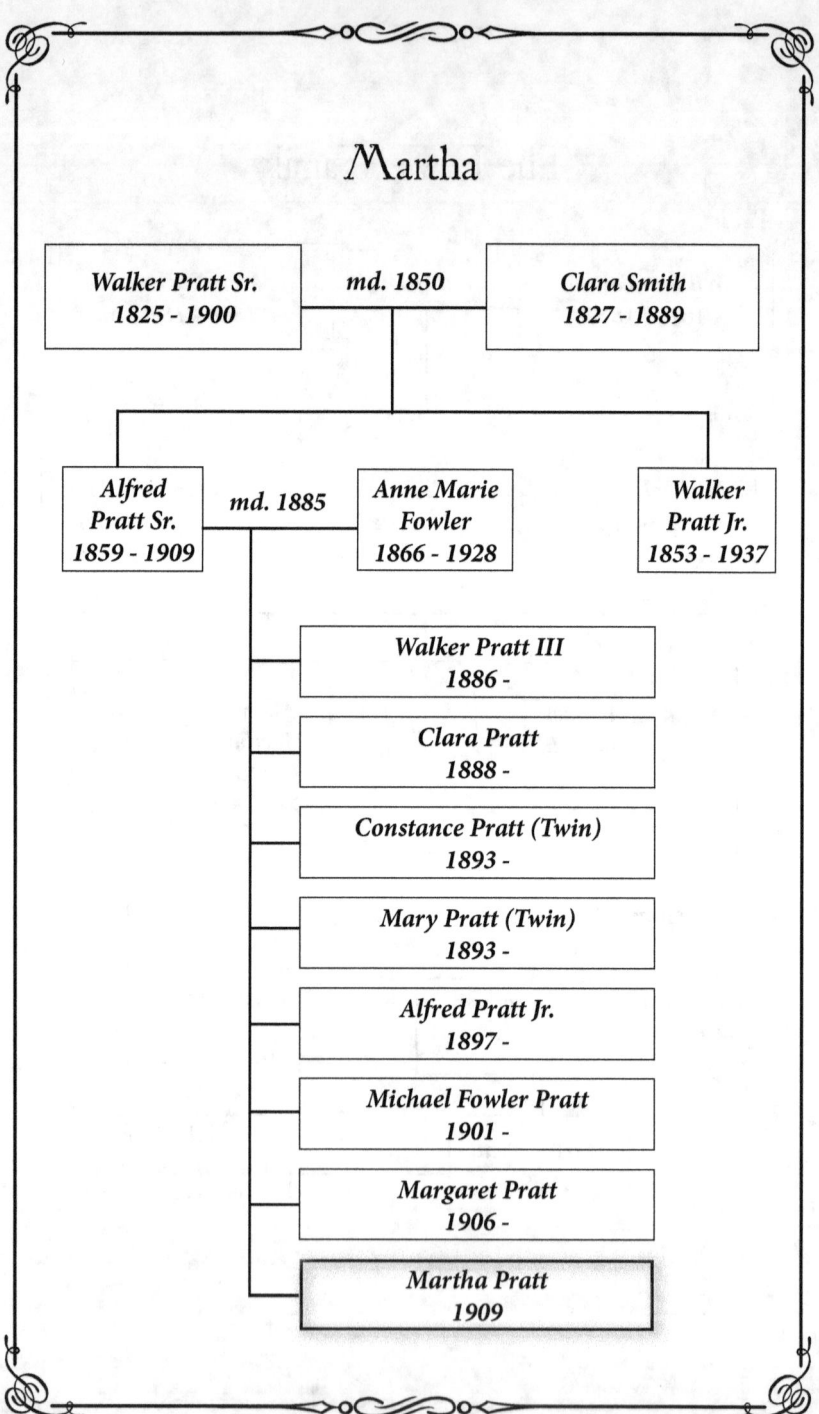

Walker Pratt Sr.
1825 - 1900

md. 1850

Clara Smith
1827 - 1889

Alfred
Pratt Sr.
1859 - 1909

md. 1885

Anne Marie
Fowler
1866 - 1928

Walker
Pratt Jr.
1853 - 1937

Walker Pratt III
1886 -

Clara Pratt
1888 -

Constance Pratt (Twin)
1893 -

Mary Pratt (Twin)
1893 -

Alfred Pratt Jr.
1897 -

Michael Fowler Pratt
1901 -

Margaret Pratt
1906 -

Martha Pratt
1909

Frank

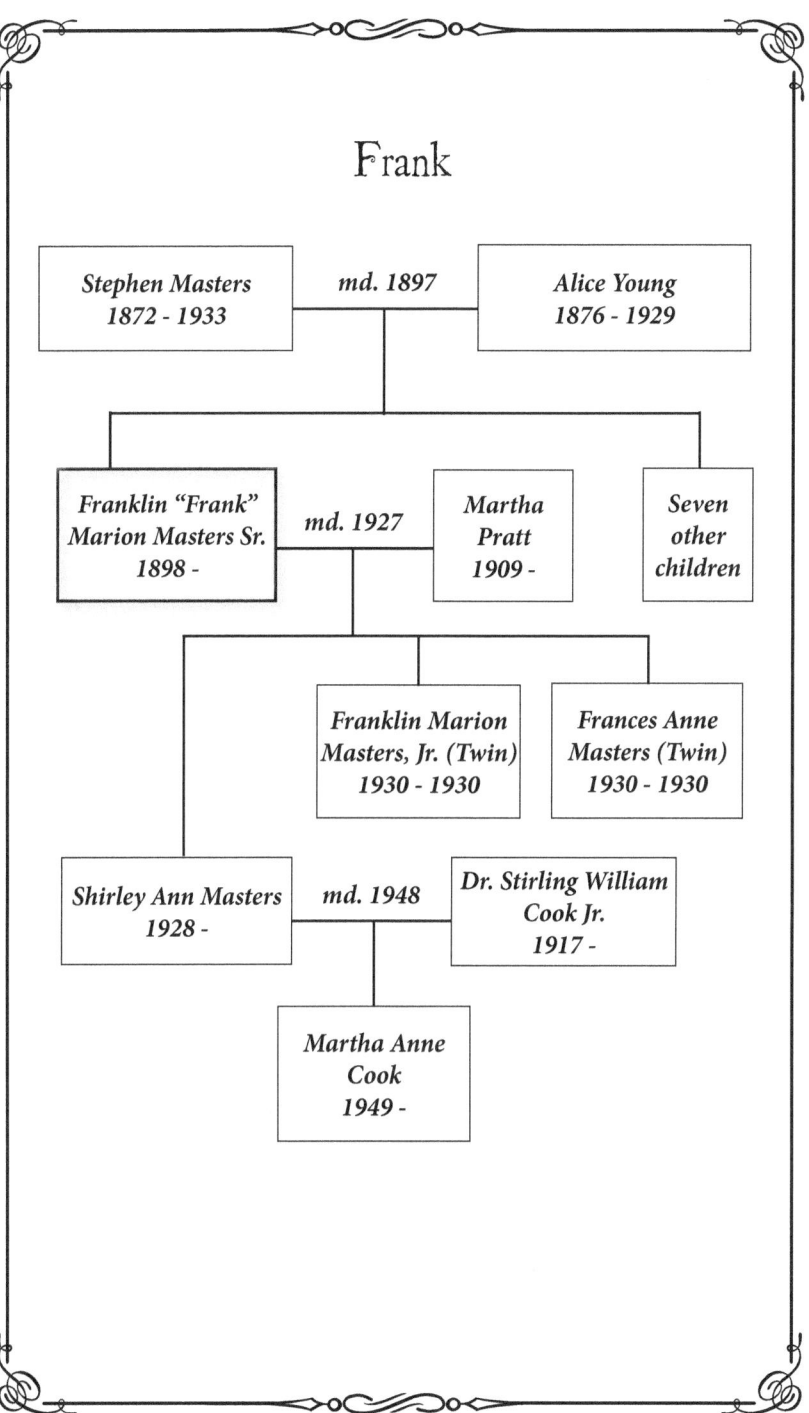

Chapter Four

————— ◦◦◦ —————

Parsons

Monday, December 24, 1883

As snow gently fell over the city of Cambridge, Massachusetts, homes were filled with laughter and merriment. Carolers could be heard throughout the community. All churches were conducting Christmas Eve services. Children were anxiously awaiting the arrival of Santa Claus.

Ten-year-old Fordham Wadsworth Parsons V always looked forward to this time of year with great anticipation. While he enjoyed the presents and all the excitement that surrounded the season, Christmas had a much deeper meaning in Fordham's life.

Fordham's mother, Mary, had taught Fordham about God at an early age. She read to him from the Bible every day. As soon as he could form words, she taught him how to pray. Each Sunday, Fordham and his mother attended services at the Congregational church. They went alone. Fordham's father, Dr. F. W. Parsons IV, was not a particularly religious man. While he acknowledged a higher authority, he was not a member of any organized church. He would not concede that Jesus Christ was anything more than a mortal man. Christmas, for Dr. Parsons, was merely another holiday.

Fordham always looked forward to Christmas Eve, when his mother read the Biblical account of the birth of Jesus Christ. This year, Fordham was more excited than ever because his mother was expecting a baby. Each night in his prayers for as long as he could remember, Fordham had asked God for a baby brother. He loved God and felt that God loved him; so there was no doubt in Fordham's mind that God would give him the brother that he wanted so badly.

Mary's pregnancy had been extremely difficult. She was forty years old and had been in frail health for several years. She remained bedridden most of her pregnancy. Fordham's father had been so concerned about Mary that he had made arrangements to have round-the-clock nursing care for her. He sought the help of Boston's finest doctors.

Fordham had no concept of the seriousness of his mother's condition. His parents wanted to shield him from any unnecessary worry. He hoped his mother would deliver his baby brother on Christmas Day. He could not think of a better Christmas present. Fordham always loved Christmas. With the new baby coming, he had a feeling that this would be the most memorable Christmas ever.

The Christmas spirit was short-lived in the Parsons home. The delivery of Mary's second son shortly before midnight was too much for Mary's frail body. She passed away during the early morning hours on Christmas Day.

An undertaker was summoned to the Parsons home. He was instructed to prepare Mary's body for burial and to place the casket containing her body in the house's library.

Fordham and his father were devastated. Mary had been the center of both their lives. Neither could imagine how he would go on without her. Visitors were turned away—even family.

Dr. Parsons attached a brief note to his front door. It said, "In mourning. No visitors, please! Dr. F. W. Parsons IV."

The many presents under the Christmas tree went unopened. Dr. Parsons instructed his butler to give them to the needy. Christmas was never again celebrated in the Parsons home.

The much bereaved Dr. Parsons rejected his infant son from the outset. He refused to see him. The baby went unnamed. A private nurse was retained to care for him. Fordham was left in the care of the family's butler and housekeeper. Instructions were given that under no circumstances was Fordham to see his baby brother.

Dr. Parsons spent the remainder of that Christmas Day alone with his Mary, reflecting back on their life together and the years of loneliness that he experienced before she entered his life.

Dr. Parsons grew up in a stately home that his father had built in 1840 on Brattle Street, in the fashionable section of Cambridge. The house became a center of Cambridge and Boston intellectual life. In his youth, Dr. Parsons was influenced by the frequent visitors to the home, which included his distant cousin, Henry Wadsworth Longfellow and Henry's wife, Fanny, who were also their neighbors. Other visitors were Nathaniel Hawthorne, Ralph Waldo Emerson, Henry David Thoreau, John Bartlett, and the controversial Bronson Alcott. Dr. Parsons would enjoy a lifelong friendship with Alcott's daughter, Louisa May.

Dr. Parsons was the third of five children born to Dr. Fordham Wadsworth Parsons III and Hannah Peabody Parsons. His father passed away in 1861. Dr. Parsons, just twenty-seven, was left with the responsibility of caring for his mother, Grandfather Parsons, and his younger siblings—Henry, age twenty, and Sarah, age fifteen—who all still lived in the family home. While most men his age had married and started their own families, Dr. Parsons was a selfless man who put the care of his family above his own needs. Marriage would have to wait.

Although he was extremely young, Dr. Parsons was invited to fill his father's chair as a professor of English literature at Harvard. As the years went by, he devoted his life to teaching, writing, and caring for his family.

Henry completed his education and accepted a position in his grandfather Henry Wilson Peabody's bank in the Boston business district. He moved into the Peabody home in nearby Chelsea.

Sarah married Joseph Whitmore in 1867. Grandfather Parsons died in his sleep in 1868, the day after his ninetieth birthday. Tragedy dealt the family a double blow on the nation's birthday in 1869, when Hannah Parsons and her eighty-five-year-old father, Henry Wilson Peabody, drowned in a boating accident in Cape Cod Bay. Dr. Parsons found himself alone in the family home for the first time in his life, with no one to care for and no one to care for him. He purchased his siblings' interest in the estate and, except for the household staff, continued to live there alone.

A man of infinite intellect and wisdom, Dr. Parsons was the type who commanded the utmost respect from his peers. His closest friends were at the top of the list of Who's Who in New England. None of them would have dared question any decision he made. However, many raised their eyebrows two years later, when thirty-seven-year-old Dr. Parsons married twenty-eight-year-old Mary Case, his housekeeper. Her background was clouded in mystery, and the marriage was not popular among the socially accepted highbrows of Cambridge and Boston.

Dr. Parsons did not dwell on what society thought of his marriage. He had looked beyond Mary's social stature and found the love and companionship he had desired for so long. His prominence outweighed the social overtones. His home continued to be a center of not only intellectual but also social activity.

Dr. Parsons stood beside his wife's casket, stared at her lifeless body, and wept. He had finally found peace and happiness in his life, only to have it taken away so quickly. He felt robbed. He had planned on spending a lifetime with Mary, but fate gave them only twelve years together. Those years seemed only moments. He wondered how God could be so cruel as to take away his beloved wife.

When darkness fell upon the city, the undertaker returned to the Parsons home. No funeral was held for Mary Case Parsons. Dr. Parsons accompanied his wife's body to her undisclosed burial location. He left instructions that the newspapers prepare no formal obituary, just a simple death notice to read: "Parsons, in this city, Dec. 25, Mary Case, beloved wife of Dr. F. W. Parsons IV, mother of Fordham. Arrangements private."

Upon his return to Cambridge one week later, Dr. Parsons paid a visit to his sister, Sarah, and her husband, Joseph. They resided in nearby Chelsea. Arrangements were made for them to take the infant and raise him in their home along with their three daughters: thirteen-year-old Hannah, nine-year-old Sophronia, and six-year-old Remember.

Sarah and Joseph chose not to formally adopt the infant. They hoped that someday Dr. Parsons would have a change of heart. Sarah and the baby's three older cousins hovered over the baby. Joseph raised him as his son. He was named Henry Wilson Parsons II after his paternal uncle, who had never married. Uncle Henry became a second father to him. The Whitmore family resided with Uncle Henry in the Peabody family home. Unfortunately, the younger Henry would never know his own father's love.

Dr. Parsons had not remained close to either of his older sisters, Remember and Prudence, after they married. He was notified when each passed away but elected not to attend either of their funerals. When Sarah and Joseph chose not to formally adopt Henry, Dr. Parsons decided to sever all relations with them. This hurt Sarah immensely, as she had always worshipped her older brother. Her choice not to formally adopt Henry was an unselfish display of affection for her brother. It did not hinder the love Sarah and Joseph showered on Henry. He called Sarah "Mama" and Joseph "Father." Sarah and Joseph's three daughters were his sisters, and he was their brother. He just had a different surname.

Henry knew of his own father's wishes and was taught to love and respect him, even if his father chose never to acknowledge him as his son. Perhaps it was the intense amount of love that was showered on him by the Whitmores and his Uncle Henry that enabled Henry to have and maintain a deep love and affection for his own father and brother. The Whitmores and Uncle Henry always spoke very highly of both Dr. Parsons and Fordham.

Dr. Parsons kept a close relationship with his brother, Henry. They had been having lunch together on the first Thursday of every month since 1861. This tradition continued even after Mary's death, with the provision that no mention be made of little Henry. This did not prevent Fordham's proud father from talking incessantly about him. Henry welcomed all news about his nephew Fordham and relayed this news to little Henry. It pained him deeply that he could not relate the accomplishments and news of little Henry to his father.

Fordham

When his mother died, ten-year-old Fordham grieved deeply and blamed God. Following his father's example, he totally rejected his younger brother. He reasoned that if Henry had not been born, his mother would still be alive.

Fordham's education began almost at birth. His parents spent a great deal of time with their son. It was no surprise to their friends that when Fordham was three, they engaged the services of private tutors to teach Fordham music, writing, reading, grammar, mathematics, art, French, German, and Latin.

One would surmise that Fordham's love of literature would come through his father, but in actuality, it was his mother who guided her son in Greek, English, French, German, and American literature. From the very beginning, Mary, who had no formal education, read to her infant son hour upon hour. Her husband had taught her to read from the books in his extensive library when she was his housekeeper. She spent all of her evenings reading late into each night. It was her intense desire to learn and her love of literature that drew Dr. Parsons to Mary. She captured his heart.

It never occurred to Mary to read children's books to her son. She was familiar only with the volumes in her husband's library, which mostly contained books of literature, history, law, language, and philosophy. Mary began reading to Fordham when he was only a few weeks old. It seemed to quiet him and gave Mary the opportunity to practice reading out loud. The many writers who frequented her home and their ability to entertain their audiences with their special readings impressed her. Additionally, Mary wanted to devote as many hours as possible to her infant son and at the same time expand her knowledge of literature. She felt it was important to be able to converse intelligently with her husband and his many prominent acquaintances.

Mary had forged a close friendship with her neighbor Henry Wadsworth Longfellow. He treated her as though she were one of his own daughters. Longfellow was very fond of Fordham from the time of his birth. Since neither of Fordham's grandfathers were living, Longfellow became his foster grandfather. Fordham called him simply "Grandfather." Fordham spent countless hours listening to Longfellow as he recited many of his own poems. Fordham's association with Longfellow left an indelible impression on Fordham and helped him develop a great love of poetry.

As the months and years went by, not only Fordham benefited from his mother's readings, but Mary did as well. She had the time to devote to her son, as his father was constantly busy teaching, lecturing, and writing. Her world would have been a lonely existence if she had not had Fordham to care for. With the exception of Longfellow, she had no personal friends other than her husband's acquaintances. It was best that way, she figured, for many reasons. That is the way she wanted it. She was devoted to her two men, and they were devoted to her.

Mary introduced her son to the writings of Sophocles, Plato, Aristotle, Chaucer, Milton, Shakespeare, Dante, Goethe, Rousseau, Burns, Emerson, Thoreau, Hawthorne, Poe, Dickens, Hugo, Alcott, Stowe, Twain, Dana, and many other poets, authors, philosophers, and historians.

From the time he was four years old, Fordham was allowed to attend all the intellectual gatherings held in the Parsons home. He was especially fond of Louisa May Alcott and her father. Louisa referred to Fordham as "my little man." When Louisa and her father died within two days of each other in 1888, Fordham felt that he had lost a beloved aunt and grandfather.

Other frequent visitors to the Parsons home included Harriett Beecher Stowe. George Bancroft, Henry Brooks Adams, Richard Henry Dana Jr., and Samuel Clemens(Mark Twain) were periodic guests. Many other prominent men and women often visited the Parsons home, since the home continued to be a center of intellectual activity. Fordham listened intently to everything the guests said and enjoyed learning from them. Their words seemed like rays of sunshine to him, and he basked in their warmth. He respected the guests' intellect and prominence, even as a small child. In turn, the guests were impressed with Fordham's impeccable manners, his astute knowledge of their writings, and his explicable ability to converse intelligently with them.

When Fordham was five years old, he was enrolled in one of

Boston's finest private schools on the condition that he could keep up with the beginning seven-year-olds. Within two weeks, he was advanced two levels and placed with the nine-year-olds. At home, his parents continued to engage the services of private tutors.

After Fordham's mother's death, Fordham's father continued to guide Fordham's education. Fordham was allowed to enroll at Harvard in the fall of 1885, when he was only twelve. He graduated with honors in 1888. He continued his studies at Oxford University in England. From there, Fordham studied at the University of Göttingen in Germany, where he was awarded a PhD in 1893. Then he spent an additional year traveling Europe, researching and writing. In 1894, Fordham accepted an offer from Bowdoin College in Brunswick, Maine, to be an instructor. He became an associate professor in 1899. Following in the footsteps of his father, Fordham accepted Harvard's offer in 1903 to be a professor of English literature, to fill the chair vacated when his father died.

Fordham was the fifth generation professor at Harvard in the family. He was the fourth generation professor at Harvard with the same name, but the legacy ended with him. There would not be a Fordham Wadsworth Parsons VI. Fordham would never marry; nor would he have or adopt any children.

Henry

When Henry Wilson Parsons II was still an infant, Sarah Whitmore began to compile an album of pictures and newspaper clippings featuring his father. She gave it to Henry on his tenth birthday, and he kept up the album on his own from that time on.

Although they lived within miles of each other, Henry never saw his father in the flesh until his father's funeral in 1903. Henry yearned for his older brother's love. He was even rejected by Fordham at their father's funeral. Henry had extended his hand

and introduced himself to his older brother: "I am your brother, Henry."

Fordham stared coldly at Henry. Seconds passed. Fordham's facial expression was somber. His eyes remained frozen on Henry's face as he replied harshly, "I have no brother!" He abruptly turned and walked away from Henry without even shaking Henry's hand.

Dr. Parsons never acknowledged Henry as his son and made Fordham his sole heir. Dr. Parsons's lengthy obituary made no mention of his second son. Thirty-two more years passed before Fordham acknowledged Henry as his brother.

Henry followed a different avenue than his father and brother. Joseph Whitmore was a partner in one of Boston's more successful law firms. He had hoped that Henry would also choose the legal profession. Being a graduate of Yale University's School of Law, Joseph was extremely pleased when Henry decided to attend his alma mater. Henry was awarded a law degree in 1907 and joined Joseph's firm. When Joseph retired in 1914, Henry was invited to become a full partner. He also replaced Joseph as a member of the board of directors of Peabody Bank and Trust, the financial institution founded in 1820 by his great-grandfather, Henry Wilson Peabody.

Uncle Henry had become chairman of the board of directors in 1869 following his grandfather's accidental death. He had been named president of the bank the previous year at age twenty-seven. It was felt within the family that due to his heavy responsibilities at the bank, Uncle Henry chose not to marry. He continued to function as both the bank's president and its chairman of the board of directors until 1911, when, at the age of seventy, he stepped down as president but remained chairman of the board of directors. At that time, Quincy Adams Hastings Jr. was named president. Quincy was the forty-three-year-old son of Uncle Henry's sister Remember. Due to poor health, Quincy resigned from his position in 1918.

Henry was offered the position. It was a difficult decision to make. Although it was Uncle Henry's desire that his nephew accept the position, he chose not to put additional pressure on him. It was Joseph Whitmore who strongly encouraged Henry to accept the bank's presidency. Joseph referred to the position as a "new challenge" in Henry's life.

Henry resigned from the law firm and accepted the bank's offer. Following Uncle Henry's death in 1923, he accepted the additional responsibility as the chairman of the bank's board of directors.

Reunion

It was a chance meeting in 1920 when Fordham was reintroduced to Katherine Uhlers, a former student and an aspiring poetess. They bonded well. He remembered her as one of his brighter students, and they became friends. She became a frequent guest in his home, which had continued to be a gathering place of fellow intellectuals and authors.

It was not until her funeral in 1935 that Fordham became aware of Katherine's secret. Katherine's personal life was totally separated from her professional life out of concern for the privacy and protection of her family. Fordham was stunned to learn that his dear friend was Mrs. Henry Wilson Parsons II, his sister-in-law and the mother of three daughters. Katherine Uhlers was her maiden name, which she also used as her pen name. Katherine's full name was a secret that Katherine had kept out of fear of losing Fordham's friendship. As a teacher, he had greatly influenced her and encouraged her to pursue her career as a poetess. As her friend, he had always been available to offer critical analysis of her poetic writings. He greatly respected her intellect and talent. It was this respect for her that prompted Katherine to continue her deceit.

At Katherine's funeral, both brothers were brought together face-to-face, and after nearly fifty-two years, the walls between them quickly fell. As the years continued on, they became close friends.

Henry's youngest daughter, Louisa, married in 1943. After that, all three daughters were married and living out of state. This left Henry alone in his spacious home in Chelsea. He was enormously wealthy and felt that it was time to retire. This allowed Quincy Adams Hastings III to replace him as both president and chairman of the board of directors at Peabody Bank and Trust. Henry resigned from both positions on his sixtieth birthday, in 1943.

Fordham suggested that Henry sell his home so he could move to Cambridge and share Fordham's spacious house. It was an offer that Henry could not decline. Sixty years previous, he was removed from the family residence because he was not wanted there. He was now asked to come home. He had waited all his life for this invitation.

Shortly after Henry moved in with Fordham, they were visiting in the library. Fordham looked pensively at Henry and said, "I believe it is time I shared the family journals with you."

The library in the Parsons home was an inspiring sight. It was a spacious room with a tall ceiling. The room was Victorian in décor. The floor was hardwood with a massive rug covering most of its surface. Four huge leather sofas and ten large, leather-cushioned chairs gave the room a feeling of warmth. There were also several writing tables. Two dozen floor lamps were positioned near the furniture throughout the room.

One wall of the library was composed entirely of windows, which allowed a sea of natural light into the room during the day. Two walls were completely filled with bookshelves from the floor to the ceiling. They contained thousands of books, which represented the complete libraries of five generations of Harvard professors in the family.

There was a fireplace in the center of the fourth wall. Surrounding the fireplace were large portraits of the Wadsworth,

Alden, and Parsons forebears. The portraits of other Parsonses, Peabodys, Graysons, Crosbys, and Hales lined the walls of the main hall of the first floor of the home. The portraits represented seven generations of the family.

Henry had spent hours studying the portraits. Missing were portraits of his mother, Mary, and brother, Fordham. When Henry had inquired of Fordham why his own portrait was not present, Fordham just chuckled and replied: "My portrait hangs in the library at Harvard. That is enough."

Fordham explained that there were no existing portraits or photographs of their mother. "Father loved Mother very deeply. His love for her knew no boundaries. After her death, he removed everything from this home that reminded him of her. He never quit loving her, but he would not share his feelings or talk openly about Mother with anyone, including me. The only exception was in his journals, where he explained his innermost thoughts and feelings."

Fordham was now about to share with Henry the family journals. Henry's heart began to beat more rapidly, as he anticipated the discoveries he would experience in them.

Henry stood in amazement as Fordham pointed out the journals of their father, grandparents, and great-grandparents and those of ancestors of earlier generations. There were eighty-nine volumes, all bound in leather. Fordham explained that he recently had many of the volumes rebound. "They have been read and reread many times. I know them well. They collect no dust!"

A smile crossed Henry's face, and he commented to Fordham: "I was taught as a child by Mother Sarah to keep a journal of my thoughts and experiences. I am presently filling my eighth volume. Katherine and I taught our children to keep journals, and they, likewise, will teach their children. Unfortunately, Joseph Whitmore never kept a journal. I wish he had. His own thoughts and personal history died with him. Mother Sarah learned to keep journals from her own parents and grandparents. She reflected many times on how when she lived here, she was able to personally know each of her forebears through reading their personal journals. My favorite bedtime stories as a child were the stories she told of her ancestors, especially the Crosbys and the Parsonses, who were mariners, and of their adventures at sea."

Fordham interjected, "Henry, there are over 250 years of family history in these volumes. I don't know of any other family so fortunate to have this much of their own history preserved. It is all here—the Aldens, the Crosbys, the Hales, the Parsonses, and the Wadsworths."

Henry added, "I have the journals of the Graysons, the McBrides, the Peabodys, the Pendletons, and the Wilsons. I will gladly share them with you and make them a part of this collection. My own wife, Katherine, started keeping a journal when she was one of your students at Harvard. She gave you the credit for teaching her the importance of keeping a personal journal. I have ten precious volumes, written in her own hand, of her memories and thoughts. Scarcely a day goes by that I don't read from them. Reading Katherine's journals helps keep the memory of her alive, and my love for her continues to grow. Her grandchildren, who never knew her personally, will someday know her when they read her journals. We have you to thank, Fordham, because you inspired her."

"No, Henry," said Fordham. "We have our great-great-grandparents to thank. They taught their children, and they, in turn, taught theirs. As I look at each of my ancestors' portraits, I feel a great debt of gratitude, not only for their words and counsel, which fill the pages of their journals, but also for the heritage they gave us. I have donated their professional correspondence to Harvard. The university recently microfilmed those journals, but I feel these original journals and the family letters should remain in the family. Someday you will pass these volumes on to one of your daughters. It will be up to you to determine which one."

Fordham further commented, "Mother kept journals also. She was the one who taught me. I remember seeing her write in her journals. After Father's death, I searched this house, but I have never located them. I suspect he burned them, as he likely did her pictures and her correspondence. Henry, it is now time that you get to know our Father."

Fordham lifted a dozen volumes from a shelf. He placed them on the small, oval-top table that stood near the chair that Henry had adopted as his favorite.

In the days that followed, Henry gained a deep insight into the father he had always loved but never knew. Henry was especially gratified as he read the entries regarding his mother. He read of his parents' courtship and of their life together. He read an entry for June 3, 1883:

> *"My beloved Mary informed me this evening that she is with child. I worry about her health. She is so fragile and has not been well for some time now. This pregnancy will not be easy on her. Yet, we are both excited and look forward with great anticipation to the birth of our second child."*

Later, Henry read the entry for December 25, 1883:

> *"My beloved is no more. Her body lies within these walls. Her precious spirit has returned from whence it came. Gone is her warmth and laughter. The touch of her hand is cold. Her cheeks are pale, and her lips are silent. I live, but my heart has been impaled. Words cannot describe my despair and grief. I feel as though I am dead, yet, I still breathe. Half of me is gone. Half of me lives on. Now, I will take my beloved home."*

There was no mention of Henry's birth. The next entry was for January 2, 1884:

"Returned to Cambridge the evening past. For young Fordham's sake I live on. Otherwise, my life is no more. I wonder, how a dead heart still beats."

Henry read on and on and on. There were numerous entries of his father's grief and heartfelt loss of his Mary. The words Henry would not speak with his family and friends were written in his journals.

When Henry came to the entry for Tuesday, March 26, 1895, a feeling of warmth rushed throughout his body.

"Took a trip to Chelsea this morning to see my son, Henry. I observed him, but he did not see me. It is best that way. He is a handsome lad. Sarah and Joseph have raised him well. I miss him. I am proud of him, and I love him. I always have, and I always will. I know I made the right decision."

This would be the only entry in Dr. Parsons's journals that would make mention of his son Henry. However, Henry was totally satisfied. He knew his father loved him, and that was all that mattered. Henry re-read this entry many times in the years that would follow. He would treasure that passage forever!

After he had completed the reading of his father's journals, Henry stood before his father's portrait in the library. He looked deep into his father's eyes. The artist had captured Dr. Parsons's true essence. The eyes showed his sincerity and his warmth. He was a man of deep conviction, and the strokes of the artist's brush did not lie. A quiet feeling of peace came over Henry. Minutes passed, and Henry continued to look upon his father's countenance. Henry said aloud, "Father, now I understand the way you dealt with your grief."

In 1950, Fordham turned seventy-seven years old. He looked younger than his age due to his healthy constitution that had not yet suffered the ravages of any debilitating illness. He was tall and handsome and had a distinguished air about him. Women found him charming but extremely aloof to any of their advances. He could sometimes be abrupt but never rude. He was an extremely formal gentleman.

The brothers enjoyed each other's company. Their only real contention came each Christmas. Although Fordham acknowledged the existence of God, from the date of his mother's death, he ignored God and separated himself from organized religion. Fordham's father and his teachers were his mentors. God was the creator, nothing further, he contended. Jesus Christ had no purpose in his life. God had removed Fordham's mother from him, the only woman he had ever loved. Perhaps it was this fear of again losing someone he loved so much that prevented him from getting married. He had no close women friends except for professional associates and acquaintances.

Henry would be sixty-seven on Christmas Eve. His appearance and personality were similar to his older brother except that Henry tended to display more warmth to strangers. Henry had no interest in remarriage. He looked closer in age to his brother than their ten-year age difference.

Henry's daughter Mary Katherine and her family lived in Providence, Rhode Island. His daughter Sarah and her family lived in Hartford, Connecticut. His youngest daughter, Louisa, resided in Swanton, Vermont, near the Canadian border.

Each year, Fordham hosted a small birthday breakfast on Christmas Eve in Henry's honor. Henry left immediately after and drove to one of his daughter's homes to celebrate Christmas. He always encouraged Fordham to come with him, and a small argument would usually ensue. Fordham had no need for Christmas. It was just another day to him. Henry always looked forward to Christmas and the opportunity to be with one of his daughters and her family. Fordham always declined the invitation, and it would not be discussed again until the next Christmas. The brothers were inseparable—except at Christmas.

Circumstances created a change this year. Henry was forced to give up driving after suffering a stroke, which left him partially paralyzed on his left side. His left arm was not much use to him anymore, and he spoke with a slight slur. His left leg had been affected, but he got along pretty well with the use of a cane. Fordham had been extremely attentive to Henry's needs during his illness and recovery. This year he elected to drive him to Swanton, Vermont, where Henry would be spending Christmas with Louisa's family. Fordham planned to return immediately and made no plans to stay over for Christmas. Henry's son-in-law Michael Cavendish would bring Henry back to Cambridge in early January. Henry was looking forward to spending time with his grandchildren: Jonah, age six, and Mary, age four. They called him Pops.

Sunday, December 24, 1950, 9:30 a.m.
The Parsons' home, Cambridge, Massachusetts

Fordham tapped a fork several times against his glass. "I would like to make a toast to my favorite brother."

Henry interrupted. "What do you mean *favorite*? I am your only brother."

Everyone laughed.

"May 1951 be a better year for you, Henry! May you enjoy improved health next year and for many years to come!"

"Thank you, big brother. I'll drink to that."

A large birthday cake with sixty-seven lighted candles was brought in and placed directly in front of Henry. Fordham led the guests in singing "Happy Birthday." After Fordham and the guests concluded, Henry smiled and said, "Fordham, it's going to take both of us to blow out that fire."

Fordham joined his brother in blowing out all the candles. Even with two of them blowing, they could not get all the candles out at once. "What has happened to me?" commented Henry. "I used to be able to blow out all my candles with breath to spare. I guess my wish won't come true this year."

"Oh, no, Henry. I wouldn't be so sure about that. Haven't you heard? They ease up on those birthday candle rules once you pass sixty-five. Everything is opposite. So even though we didn't get all the candles blown out, your wish just might come true."

"Well, Fordham, I hope that's true, because my wish was that you would spend Christmas with me this year."

"Sorry, Henry. You know wishes don't come true if you tell what you wished for."

"What about the after sixty-five rules? It seems to me you said something about the rules being opposite. Looks as though you'll be spending Christmas with me this year after all, Fordham. You had better go pack your bag."

Everyone seemed to enjoy the sparring between the two brothers.

"Okay, okay, you got me there. I made the whole thing up. Now, little brother, you have some presents to open."

Henry opened up a box that contained a new cane with a personalized inscription from Fordham: "To my best friend and brother, Henry Wilson Parsons II, on the occasion of his sixty-seventh birthday, December 24, 1950. With deepest affection, Fordham Wadsworth Parsons V."

As Henry read the inscription, his eyes filled with tears. This was the most touching gift Henry had ever received from Fordham. Henry was so moved that it was difficult for him to speak; yet he wanted to express his deep appreciation to his dear brother. He tried to choke back the tears. "Thank you, Fordham. You have no idea what this means to me." It was some time before Henry was able to fully regain his composure.

Henry continued opening the packages his guests placed before him. After he opened the last gift, he expressed his gratitude to all. "Thank you all for being so kind and thoughtful. Please excuse Fordham and me. We'd better get on the road before the snow gets worse."

Later

"Fordham, please reconsider and spend Christmas with us. It will be well past midnight when you get back to Cambridge. I worry that you will be too tired to make it home safely."

"Hush, Henry. I can't concentrate on the road with your chatter. The snow is getting worse."

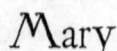

Mary

A knock came at my door one day.
  "Is the master in?" The young lady was heard to say.
"You need a housekeeper, the advertisement read."
  "Yes, he is, and yes, we do." My butler said.
Like a breath of fresh air, she entered my life.
  She touched my heart. She became my wife.

"I carry a hurt," she told me one day.
  "It's buried deep within my heart, and there it must stay."
"Please, help me to master my pain and my grief."
  "Oh, yes, I will," I promised, to her relief.
Hand in hand, we went forward happily.
  Soon we were blessed, and two became three.

Her burden was lightened, but tears still came her way.
  "Please, God, forgive me," I often heard her pray.
Many times at night, unable to sleep, she arose from our bed
  Alone with her thoughts, often she read.
Comfort she sought, and wisdom she gained.
  The words of the authors and poets, seemed to ease her pain.

Unmatched beauty and warmth, within and without, she possessed.
  And all those who met her were deeply impressed.
Unparalleled joy and happiness we shared. Our love soared.
  Then, in an instant, death came to our door.

My beloved is no more. Her body lies within these walls.
   Her precious spirit has returned from whence it came.
Gone is her warmth and laughter. The touch of her hand is cold.
   Her cheeks are pale, and her lips are silent.
I live, but my heart has been impaled.
   Words cannot describe my despair and grief.
I feel as though I am dead, yet, I still breathe.
   Half of me is gone. Half of me lives on.

I wonder, how a dead heart still beats!

Journal entry of Dr. F. W. Parsons IV
January 10, 1884

Fordham & Henry

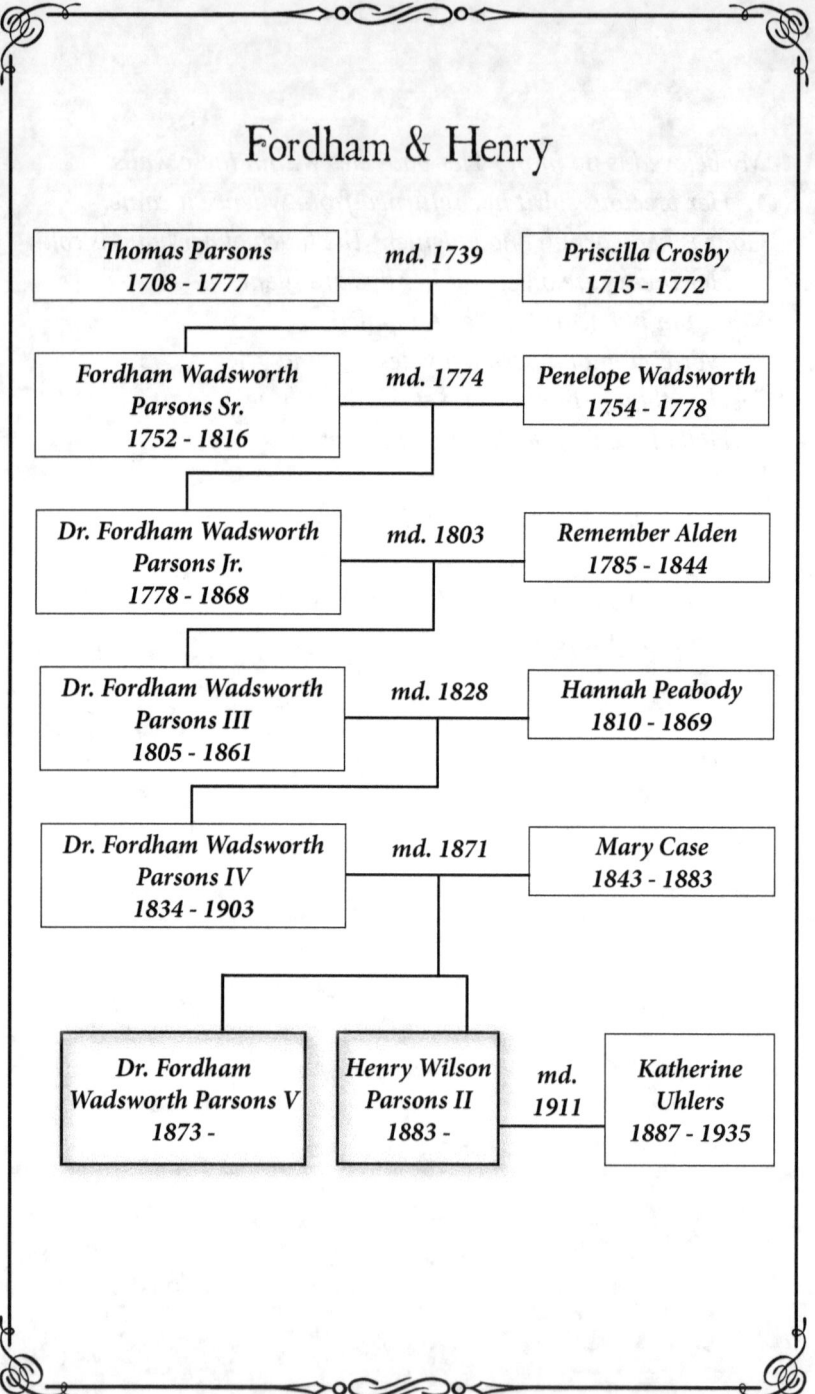

| Thomas Parsons 1708 - 1777 | md. 1739 | Priscilla Crosby 1715 - 1772 |

| Fordham Wadsworth Parsons Sr. 1752 - 1816 | md. 1774 | Penelope Wadsworth 1754 - 1778 |

| Dr. Fordham Wadsworth Parsons Jr. 1778 - 1868 | md. 1803 | Remember Alden 1785 - 1844 |

| Dr. Fordham Wadsworth Parsons III 1805 - 1861 | md. 1828 | Hannah Peabody 1810 - 1869 |

| Dr. Fordham Wadsworth Parsons IV 1834 - 1903 | md. 1871 | Mary Case 1843 - 1883 |

| Dr. Fordham Wadsworth Parsons V 1873 - | Henry Wilson Parsons II 1883 - | md. 1911 | Katherine Uhlers 1887 - 1935 |

Chapter Five

Emory

"Jan, Jan, please..." Logan Emory was having a difficult time getting his fiancée's attention over the telephone.

"Logan, it's our wedding gift from Daddy. He'll be so disappointed if we don't accept."

"We'll talk later. If I don't leave soon, I won't make it to Stowe until this evening." Logan knew what he did not want, and that was to be indebted to Julius Sommers.

The Sommers hotel chain included some of the finest hotels in the world: the Victoria in London, the Palms in West Palm Beach, the St. Sebastian in San Francisco, the Park in New York City, and the Sommers in Chicago. There was also the Sommers department store chain: twenty-six major department stores in the largest cities in the United States. Julius Sommers owned them all, and he owned people. Logan did not want to be one of those people. He was not interested in Sommers' wealth, nor was he impressed by it. He was not marrying Julius Sommers; he was marrying his daughter.

The wedding gift that Logan did not want was a thirty-two-room mansion, which Jan had located and talked her father into buying. Along with the mansion would come the money to operate it, strings Logan did not want or need.

Harrison Logan Emory III was born in 1919 into one of New England's most prominent families. His great-grandfather was a general in the Union army during the Civil War. Logan's grandfather and great-great-grandfather had been governors. His great-uncle was a US senator, and his father was currently serving on the US Supreme Court. Logan had already distinguished himself as Boston's youngest sitting judge.

Fortunately for Logan, the Sommers family resided in Florida and spent most of their time there. Jan went to Brown University, and her roommate was Catherine Mary Emory, Logan's youngest sister. Catherine invited Jan to spend part of her summer vacation at the Emory home in Arlington, Virginia. Logan was also there on vacation. That was when he first met Jan.

It was Christmas Eve 1950. Logan would be driving alone from Boston to Stowe, Vermont. He was meeting Jan and some friends for Christmas and a skiing vacation.

Life

The journey of life, uncertain in the beginning,
Is short for some and long for others.
Some are given a good road map;
While others have no map at all.

Some are born into good and wholesome homes.
Others seem destined from the start to fail.
Some wallow in their wealth,
While others rise above their poverty.

Wealth and poverty are not
True yardsticks of success or failure.
Success is measured by one's actions,
And what is in one's heart.

Success without love,
Is not true success!
A life without love,
Is no life at all!

Journal entry of Logan Emory
May 4, 1974

Chapter Six

The Storm

Sunday, December 24, 1950

It was exactly 253 miles from Laura Winchester's apartment in Boston to her parents' home in St. Albans, Vermont. She had made this trip many times over the years. Laura had always looked forward to going home. This time the feeling was different. Hope and excitement were in the eyes of her children. It was Christmas Eve, and they could hardly wait for Santa's arrival. Laura's heart was nearly broken. Her children's Christmas presents remained behind the locked door of Sullivan's Toy Shop in Boston. She tried to fill her mind with other thoughts as she made her way up Route 3 through Manchester and Concord, New Hampshire.

Laura headed northwest on Route 4 just after she drove through Boscawen. She crossed over into Vermont and continued on Route 14 through Sharon and up to Barre, where she would head west to Montpelier. As she left Barre, Laura noticed that it was five minutes past four in the afternoon. *It will be dark very soon*, she thought. Just seventy-three miles to go! The children were asleep. The sun was setting.

Laura had not seen any snowflakes fall for hours and was thankful for good road conditions. She turned on the car radio and located a familiar Burlington station. She would take Route 2 just before Montpelier and then on to Burlington. From there she would head north up Route 7 for the last twenty-eight miles to St. Albans.

Bing Crosby's "White Christmas" was playing over the radio. It really is a white Christmas, Laura thought, as a hint of a smile crossed her face. The song reminded her of the first Christmas she and Samuel had spent together. As special memories flooded her mind, she forgot about her present problem. Her memories faded when the music was interrupted with a traffic alert. The radio announcer stated that snow was falling heavily in central and northwestern Vermont. The snow mixed with freezing rain and sleet could be very dangerous. Motorists were advised to use extreme caution.

As Laura exited Montpelier, it began to snow again. It was 4:20 p.m. She passed through Middlesex. Just sixty miles to go, she thought. Traffic had slowed to twenty-five miles per hour, and visibility was getting worse. Laura tried to stay calm. As she was about to enter the village of Waterbury, she heard another traffic alert. A number of roads were now closed.

No problem, Laura thought. *I'll alter my course and head north on Route 100 and drive through Stowe, which is always very picturesque at this time of the year. I'll continue north to Morristown and head west to St. Albans.* Having traveled these roads many times before, she knew that this route was only six miles longer.

About six miles later, visibility was getting even worse. Even though traffic had slowed to ten miles per hour, Laura struggled to remain calm. Since Laura could see only a few yards ahead, she concentrated on following the taillights of the motorist in front of her. The wind gusts were very strong, and traffic slowed to five miles per hour. *Everything is going to be fine*, Laura told herself, trying not to feel fear or worry. Then the motorist in front of her came to a complete halt. She could not see beyond his vehicle.

Laura waited several very long minutes. She noticed the people behind her got out of their vehicle and walked ahead. A few minutes later, a young man tapped on her window, and she rolled it down.

"I think we've got a problem, ma'am. A large tree has fallen across the road two vehicles ahead, and now a tree has fallen behind us. It appears no one is hurt, but until a road crew can get up here to remove the trees, we are going nowhere. It's best to stay in your car and keep warm. The wind is very strong—about fifty miles per hour, I estimate."

Laura quickly rolled up her window, not wanting to let any more cold air in. The children were still asleep. Five very long minutes passed. The snow was falling heavily now. She heard several more trees fall. The howling of the wind was near deafening. She was surprised it did not wake the children. She felt restless in the car, and since the children were still sleeping, she decided to get out and investigate the situation.

Laura pushed hard to open her car door against the pressure of the strong wind. She noticed a small group of people forming. There were five vehicles, including hers, trapped by the fallen trees. Approaching vehicles were turning around and heading in opposite directions. No one was able to communicate the five cars' plight to any of these cars. The group was trying to decide what course of action to take. They were concerned that trees near their vehicles might also topple at any given moment.

The group noticed a small light off to the west coming their way. A sleigh pulled by one horse soon arrived. A young man, who appeared to be in his early twenties, drove it. He was carrying a kerosene lantern. The group quickly advised him of their situation. More trees were heard falling in the distance. The young man introduced himself as Ethan and said he was from the village of Ashton, just west of them.

Ethan advised the group that the road to Ashton was open, and everyone was welcome to stay at the Bradford Inn until the road was cleared. As the group heard more trees toppling in the distance, all agreed to follow Ethan. Members of the group asked if there was a road connecting Ashton with Stowe, Waterbury, or Waterbury Center. Ethan replied that the only road to and from Ashton was the one that he had just traveled.

No one had noticed the small road to Ashton prior to Ethan's arrival. Nor had anyone taken notice of the sign pointing toward Ashton. Yes, there was an opening in the trees, but snow covered all traces of any road, and visibility was too poor to notice the sign or any evidence of the road.

As the caravan of five automobiles made its way slowly behind the sleigh, Laura felt a calming peace filter through her body. A vast forest of trees bordered the small road, but none of the trees had fallen. When the five cars came out of the forest, Laura noticed that it was 5:38 p.m. The fierce wind gusts had subsided. Snow had ceased to fall, and the evening air did not seem very cold at all. A full moon was visible. Laura could not believe the total change in weather conditions. It seemed as though she had stepped from one world into another. It seemed lighter than it should be for that time of evening. Visibility was clear in all directions. Laura and everyone else noticed the beautiful, quaint village of Ashton a short distance away, among fields of clear white snow and nestled against a mountain of snow-covered trees.

A Winter Storm

Thunder, lightning, rain, flood,
Sleet, hail, snow and ice.
Fierce wind, bitter cold,
Elements of a winter storm.

Fallen trees, power lines down,
Bridges out and roads closed.
Lives disrupted: an hour, a day,
A week, a month or more.

Perhaps, lives never to be
The same again!

Journal entry of Logan Emory
Feb 28, 1951

Chapter Seven

Bradford Inn

At the edge of the village of Ashton was a very large two-story inn, painted white with green trim. The inn was decorated for Christmas with many green wreaths and big, beautiful red bows.

The Bradford Inn was a welcome sight. As the caravan came to a halt in front of the inn, an elderly, but very stately, gentleman appeared at the top of the front steps. He was waving for everyone to come in. He had an air of dignity and exactness about him.

Laura was the first of the group to appear at the entrance of the inn. "I am Laura Winchester, and these are my children, Sam and Sara."

"Welcome to the Bradford Inn. I am your host, Dr. Bradford Allen. My daughter Patience, will show you to the drawing room."

A polite young girl appeared and escorted Laura and her children to a very large room. It was much different from any room Laura had ever seen. It was filled with large leather chairs and sofas. Although spacious, it seemed very homelike. There was a huge hearth that kept the room well heated. The inner wall contained several paintings of persons who appeared to have lived in the 1800s, or perhaps even the 1700s, Laura surmised. There were a lot of Christmas decorations, all appearing to be homemade. There was a big, beautiful Christmas tree in one corner. It was different from any Laura had ever seen. There were no lights on the tree, just homemade ornaments and candles. The floor of the room was hardwood, and there were a number of homespun rugs throughout the room.

The furniture all appeared to be from the 1800s or perhaps earlier. The outer side of the long room was completely made up of windows. The view of the countryside was picturesque. There were no blinds or curtains framing the windows. The strongest impression Laura had was that she was at home. She felt warmth, inner peace, and love in this room. She wished time could stop and that this very moment could continue forever.

Patience escorted two elderly gentlemen into the room. "I am Henry Parsons, and this is my brother, Dr. Fordham Parsons." Laura introduced herself and her children to the Parsons.

As the Winchesters and the Parsons were becoming acquainted, Patience brought a middle-aged couple into the drawing room. They introduced themselves as Martha and Frank Masters.

A young couple, Johnny and a very pregnant Molly Maverick, entered the room. As Johnny introduced himself and his wife, both Henry Parsons and Frank Masters chimed in unison, "Johnny Maverick of the Boston Braves?"

Molly saved the moment and prevented additional unwanted questions by explaining, "My husband had the privilege of playing with the Braves for several years. He also had the honor to serve his country during the war. He is presently enjoying the opportunity to teach and coach in high school."

The last guest to appear in the drawing room and introduce

himself was the young man Laura remembered. He was the one who had appeared at her car window not quite an hour ago. The young man entered the room as Molly was explaining about Johnny. The young man was tall and handsome and seemed to command respect. "Logan Emory," he said, as he held out his hand and made everyone's acquaintance.

Dr. Parsons asked, "Any relation to Justice Harrison Logan Emory of the United States Supreme Court?"

"My father!" Logan replied firmly.

Henry Parsons spoke next. "I am an old acquaintance of your father and of his father, the governor, and his grandfather, the general. My bank had the pleasure of their business. You, sir, have an illustrious pedigree."

"Thank you," Logan replied, being a bit embarrassed and grateful that Henry Parsons had not mentioned his two great-uncles, the senator and the state supreme court justice, as well as his great-great-grandfather, Governor Edward Phineas Emory.

Henry further inquired, "You are a judge also, I understand?"

"I was appointed to the bench last year," Logan replied reluctantly. He wanted to change the subject and was hoping that someone would come to his rescue.

Laura was impressed, but somehow she felt out of place. All of these people were persons of stature in their communities. They all held positions of importance and respect. She felt socially inferior to them. She quietly hoped that no one would ask her any questions about her background, especially her ancestry.

Both Logan and Laura were totally relieved when Dr. Allen entered the room and said, "I want everyone to feel at ease and to enjoy my home as though it were your own. I am sorry that you have all been inconvenienced due to the bad weather and the terrible road conditions. My family and I will do everything we can to make your visit with us a pleasant one until the highways can be cleared.

"Unfortunately, Ashton is a bit of an old-fashioned community. The twentieth century has not quite caught up with us. We have no modern conveniences: telephones, televisions, radios, telegraph, electricity, running water, or indoor toilets. We are sorry that we have no way for you to personally contact your loved ones. However, I do have a strong feeling that every one of them will know that you are safe and will be joining them as soon as the weather and road conditions permit.

"I would like to introduce my family to you. As I mentioned earlier, I am Dr. Bradford Allen, and I am eighty-five years young. I am old enough to have delivered nearly everyone who presently lives in Ashton. This is my daughter Millicent and her grandchildren: Ethan, Sabrina, and Mary. It is worth noting that Millicent's mother was a woman of exquisite beauty and charm, both of which Millicent inherited. Unfortunately, her mother was taken from me many years ago. Thirteen years ago, my second wife and I became the parents of Patience. Sadly, my second wife died five years ago. Keeping up with Patience has kept me young, active, and busy. And I have had trouble finding time for my other patients."

Laughter filled the room. Everyone immediately felt at peace, as though they were at home.

Dr. Allen continued, "It is my pleasure to introduce to you a very special young lady, with whom I had the pleasure of becoming acquainted some time ago, when I delivered her. Constance is betrothed to my great-grandson Ethan. She will be the mother of my great-great-grandchildren, and I expect to deliver every one of them."

Laughter again filled the room.

All eyes continued to focus on Dr. Allen. When the laughter subsided, the broad smile that brightened his worn, but still handsome, face faded. Several moments passed. Dr. Allen's face took on an expression of seriousness. His eyes surveyed the faces of each of his guests.

"I am very proud of my family," stated Dr. Allen. "All of my family! I doubt there is a man on earth who loves his family more than I do. I have gone to great lengths and great depths for my family's well-being. I know all their heartaches, and if it is within my power, I will continue to do everything I can to ensure their happiness."

All felt the seriousness of the moment. Many had tears in their eyes. Everyone was touched greatly by the love and the eloquence of the aged patriarch.

Why do I feel this way? Laura wondered. *Why do I feel this overwhelming, wonderful blanket of love, warmth, and peace? Why do I feel all of my problems do not exist anymore?* She could not find the answers. Somehow, she was at total peace, and she never wanted this moment or this feeling to end.

Dr. Allen continued, "This time of year is always very special to us here in the village of Ashton. Nearly every one of our townsfolk was in church this morning as we worshiped our Lord and Savior. He suffered a horrible death that we might enjoy a wondrous, everlasting life. On this Christmas Eve, we are reminded especially of his divine birth and the gift of life, which he so freely gave to each of us. We are also reminded of the wise men and their visit to the Christ Child to present their precious gifts of gold, frankincense, and myrrh to honor him. I believe that is why we exchange Christmas presents with those we love. They are in remembrance of the precious gifts of the wise men to our Savior and of the precious gifts that the Lord has given to all of us who honor him. I give to each of you the most precious of gifts I can on this special occasion. I share with each of you my home, my family, and our love."

Fordham Parsons swallowed hard. He was deeply touched. For sixty-seven years, he had tried to forget Jesus Christ and especially the story of His birth. Now he was recalling the story of the birth of Christ, the story his mother read to him each Christmas Eve. No! He must forget all of this. Why should he celebrate the birth of Christ when God so cruelly took his dear, sweet mother away from him? His mother loved God, believed in God, and trusted him, but she was only deceived by him! Fordham sat erect and fought hard to hold his composure, but inside, he was losing the battle.

Frank Masters reached for Martha's hand and whispered the words, "I love you." She looked up at him in surprise as a wave of warmth swept through her body.

No one had noticed the departure of Millicent and her girls, Constance, Sabrina, and Mary. Those in the drawing room heard three strokes of a bell coming from the direction of the dining room. Dr. Allen announced that dinner was ready and invited all to join him.

Never in her life had Laura seen so much food. There was enough to feed her family for several months. Millicent placed an extremely large turkey in the center of the very wide and lengthy table. There was also a large ham and a beef roast on the table. Rolls, butter, jellies, cranberry sauce, potatoes, yams, gravies, and vegetables filled the serving bowls, and all were filled to the brim. It was as though the guests had been expected.

Dr. Allen invited all to sit down and requested that they hold hands. He gave a most eloquent blessing on the food.

When everyone thought they could eat no more, Millicent and her girls brought out trays of pies, puddings, sweet breads, cookies, homemade candies, and nuts.

Logan Emory was drawn to Laura. He was pleasantly surprised when Dr. Allen seated him next to her at the dining table. Laura was the complete opposite of Jan. Jan was very socially oriented and planned every word she said to maximize its effect. This both amused and irritated Logan. Laura's conversation was fresh and alive. Logan was very much at ease when he was talking with her. With Jan, he was always on his guard. Logan had known Laura for only a couple of hours, but he already knew that she was very special.

Logan began to question any feelings he had ever felt for Jan. Now he was not sure he had known what love was. He was thirty-one years old and had dated a lot of women over the years. Logan had always been careful not to date the same woman too often. This was his way of not getting too close too soon. It had always worked until he met Jan. She had a controlling personality and had completely taken over their dating schedule and, before long, his complete social schedule. She did not seem to understand the word no. However, Logan enjoyed being with her and the challenge of trying to figure out her next move.

Jan was the first woman Logan had ever allowed to invade his personal space. She was funny, beautiful, charming, vibrant, and vivacious. In public, Logan and Jan seemed to make the perfect pair. Logan had thought love was a practical thing. Logan knew that Jan would handle her role well as the wife of a judge.

Logan reflected that he had never asked Jan to marry him. The wedding was her idea, and he was just going along with it— until now! He had never told Jan he loved her. Come to think of it, she had never said the words "I love you" to him either. Logan then concluded that he and Jan were not in love. Until now, that did not matter. He and Jan were on a roller coaster ride going nowhere. Logan finally realized it. Now he wanted to get off. He knew he could never go through with his wedding to Jan. Not now—not ever!

No woman had ever affected Logan as Laura did. He had never experienced the stirring of his emotions this way. He was a judge. He understood people, their motives and reactions. He was guilty of being totally smitten in just a few hours. This surprised him most of all. Logan had never known this wonderful, warm feeling before. However, he was certain that this feeling he had for Laura was love.

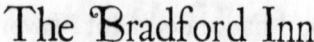

The Bradford Inn

When I think of Christmas,
I think, first, of the Christ Child, and His birth,
Of Joseph and Mary, turned from the inn,
A stable, a manger and animals around,
Of shepherds, in the fields, who followed the star,
Of the Wise Men bringing precious gifts for their King.

When I think of the Bradford Inn,
I think, first, of it being a place of refuge
And comfort for any weary, worn traveler.
I know that strangers will not be turned away.
I think of Dr. Bradford Allen, his family,
The love in their hearts and their willingness to share.

What more fitting place for a stranded traveler
To spend the Christmas holiday,
Than as a welcome guest of the doctor and his family
At the Bradford Inn in Ashton, Vermont?
I know that Joseph, Mary and their baby
Would have been welcome there too!

Journal entry of Molly Maverick
November 21, 1960

Dr. Allen & His Family

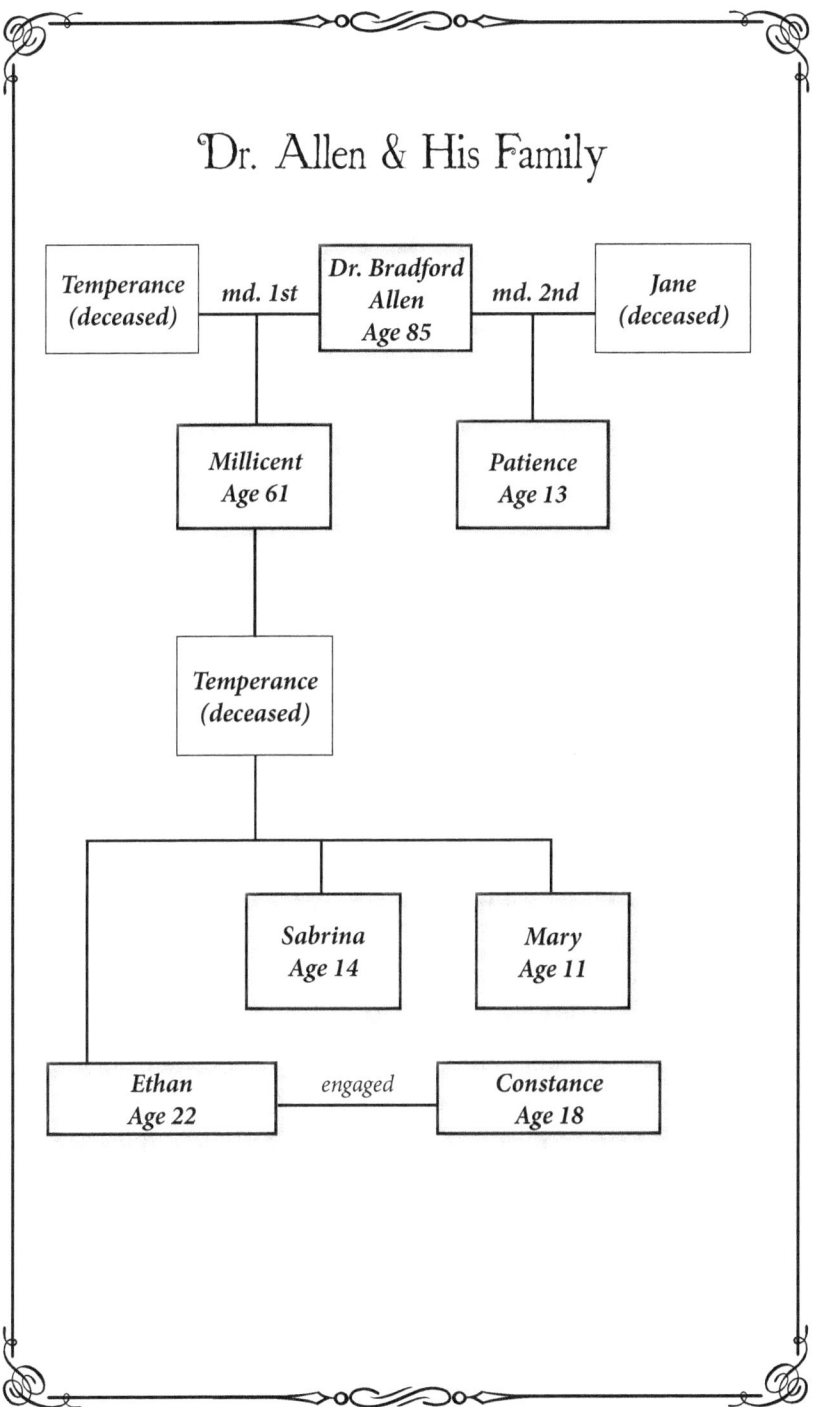

Chapter Eight

The Carolers

Dr. Allen's family and their guests heard carolers outside the inn. All the dinner guests and their hosts arose and went out onto the front porch. The evening air was pleasant, not too cold. There was a large group of carolers. It seemed as though the entire village were there. The brilliance of many lanterns coupled with the full moon gave the semblance of day, rather than night.

Henry looked at his pocket watch... 7:37 p.m. He glanced around at all of his newfound friends and noticed that there was a special, almost hallowed, glow about Dr. Allen. He radiated with peaceful happiness unmatched by anyone Henry had ever known in his sixty-seven years.

Little eleven-year-old Mary had wedged herself between Henry and Fordham. She took Henry's large left hand in her small right hand. She was holding Fordham's right hand with her left hand. A smile crossed Fordham's face. Henry was also deeply drawn to this small child without knowing why.

Fordham was really enjoying the songs of the carolers. For sixty-seven years, he had refused to celebrate Christmas. He could not believe he was allowing himself to enjoy this moment. It was as though all the pain of that dreaded event sixty-seven years previous had subsided.

Fordham relished the attention little Mary was giving him. This was out of character for Fordham, as he was not used to children. They had never been a part of his life. It was difficult for him to understand all the things that had happened or were happening to him, especially the emotions he was feeling during these last few hours in Ashton.

Fordham noticed a pleasant, familiar-looking couple among the carolers. When had he seen them before? Not recently, he surmised. *Yes, that's it*, he thought. They must have been students in one of my classes at Harvard. They were older now, and he could not quite place them. Then, he thought he saw... *No, it couldn't be*, he thought. Fordham searched the crowd. *It was just an illusion*, he surmised and quickly dismissed the thought from his mind.

Constance and Molly were sitting on the porch swing, enjoying the carolers. Ethan and Johnny were standing directly behind them. Thirteen-year-old Patience found a spot next to Molly. Patience seemed pleased when Molly put her arm around her. Molly was ready to deliver any day now, but she was hoping the baby would wait until the due date, December 29. Molly would be safely in Winooski by then.

Patience seemed to sense the delivery date was near. "Picked out any names yet?" she inquired.

Molly smiled and replied, "If it's a girl, we'll name her Rachel, after my mother. My mother died when I was a year old. If it's a boy, Johnny will name it, and he hasn't chosen a name yet." It must have been a good answer, as Molly noticed a big smile on Patience's face.

Molly was really enjoying the singing of the carolers—and the moment. The cold night air felt good, and everything seemed perfect.

Molly noticed two of the carolers looking directly at her. They were both women. She could not see the face of one of the women since a muffler covered most of it and only her forehead and eyes were visible. Molly noticed pain in the woman's eyes, which caused her to feel compassion for the woman. The other woman became aware that Molly had noticed them staring at her, whereupon a smile appeared on her face. Then she approached Molly and placed a small wooden box in Molly's hands. The lady said softly to Molly, "I would like you and your baby to have this."

Molly was surprised by the gift. A faint "thank you" fell from her lips but was not heard because the lady had quickly gone.

Molly looked down at the small wooden box. She pushed away the metal clasp. As she opened the box, she beheld a beautiful, silver antique locket, which glistened in the light of the many lanterns. Inside the locket were two small, oval pictures. One was of a young girl not more than fifteen or sixteen years of age. The second picture was of a baby. Molly had never seen these pictures before and sensed that the locket was of great value to the lady who gave it to her. For some reason, the woman had wanted Molly and her baby to have it, and Molly would treasure the generous gift. The woman who placed the box in Molly's hands was in her thirties, and Molly surmised that these were pictures of her as a young mother with her baby. *Why?* Molly wondered. *Why would she part with such a meaningful personal treasure? Why would she want to give it to my baby and me?* Molly was deeply touched.

Molly tried to locate the two women again among the carolers. Thoroughly searching the group with her eyes, she failed to locate them.

Logan sensed that fourteen-year-old Sabrina might have a crush on him. She was standing next to him while he was enjoying the carolers. He put his left arm around her to help her keep warm. He had his right arm around Laura, who did not seem to mind one bit. Samuel and Sara were occupied as Dr. Allen had them seated with him on a porch bench.

Martha and Frank Masters were especially drawn to the faces of two carolers, both appeared to be about nineteen or twenty years of age, a young man and a young woman. Frank noticed how much the young lady looked like Martha. Martha noticed how much the young man looked like Frank. Both Frank and Martha kept their thoughts to themselves. Martha remarked to Frank, "Never have I ever heard such beautiful music. It is as though we are listening to a heavenly choir."

Frank also reflected. Never in his life had he heard such inspired caroling. This was indeed the largest group of carolers he had ever seen assembled at one time. *The carolers must think highly of Dr. Allen and his family*, he concluded. The carolers sang a final carol, one Frank had never heard before.

As the carolers departed, Martha noticed a woman, who appeared to be in her midthirties, leading Martha's two favorite carolers away. Martha assumed the woman was their mother. Then the woman looked back at the guests at the inn. For a moment, Martha thought she was looking at her own mother at an age much younger than she remembered. *No! It couldn't be*, she concluded. Then the woman turned away. A warm feeling rushed through Martha's body. At the same time, Frank received the same impression, even though he and Martha did not share their feelings with each other.

"We have been greatly honored," noted Dr. Allen to his guests. "Will you all join me in the drawing room?"

The Carolers

It was not the carols
   Which they sang that night.
It was not the music or the words
   Which touched our hearts.

The carolers sang in the cool night air,
   Inspiring messages of Christmas joy.
Their countenances aglow, radiated with love,
   Reminded us of a heavenly, angelic choir.

With a hunger to serve, they both blessed
   And honored us with their presence.
It was the love they seemed to have for us,
   And their hearts touched ours.

Journal entry of Frank Masters
January 6, 1955

Chapter Nine

Ashton

Logan remained on the porch alone. He had informed Laura that he would join her and the others in a few minutes. He looked out over the village of Ashton. The carolers could be seen entering their own homes. *What a quaint little village,* he reflected. It was so peaceful and so removed from the big-city life he was used to. For a moment, he envied Dr. Allen and the other residents of Ashton.

Logan looked at his watch. It was eight o'clock in the evening. With the sky so clear and peaceful now and the full moon reigning majestically over the village, he had forgotten, for the moment, the plight that he and the other guests were experiencing. He walked briskly to his new Cadillac sedan. His radio dial was still set on the Montpelier station, which he had been listening to at the time the road was blocked.

The newscaster reported that many of the roads in the area were still impassable. Heavy amounts of snow and ice, followed by fierce winds, had resulted in the toppling of a large number of trees and power lines. No one knew when road and power company crews would be able to clear the roads. It was reported that snow was still falling and would continue throughout the night. Logan found that odd since the sky was so clear over Ashton. It was a beautiful evening with all the stars visible. The newscaster reported that that there were no known casualties, and he advised motorists of the road closings. He also reported the sighting of Santa Claus so children would not worry. Santa and his reindeer appeared to be on schedule.

Logan entered the drawing room, where the others had regathered, except for Millicent and her girls. They were busy in the kitchen and dining room. Logan reported the current road conditions to the others.

Dr. Allen addressed his guests. "Once again, I am sorry that all of you have been inconvenienced. There are plenty of beds for everyone. This is a big inn, you know. It is not necessary for any of you to register for rooms. This is also my home. You are all my guests, and it is Christmas.

"The nearest telegraph office that is open this Sabbath evening is at the radio station in Waterbury. Since the road is closed, Ethan will hook up his sleigh and use a trail he is familiar with. He will send messages to your loved ones to let them know you are safe and will join them as soon as the weather and roads permit."

Names and addresses were collected from the guests of those to be notified. Laura was grateful for this since she knew her parents would be relieved to know that she, Samuel, and Sara were all right and among friends.

Frank and Martha knew their daughter and son-in-law would be pleased to know that all was well with them. There was a peace and contentment that they were both feeling. They were enjoying their first real happiness together in many years.

Henry missed being with his grandchildren. However, Samuel and Sara reminded him of his four-year-old granddaughter, Mary, and his six-year-old grandson, Jonah.

Eleven-year-old Mary had finished her kitchen chores and was sitting between Fordham and Henry on a sofa in the drawing room. *This will be a very enjoyable Christmas*, Henry concluded. Henry noticed that Fordham had placed his arm around Mary's shoulder and had pulled her close to him. This surprised Henry, as this was very out of character for his brother.

Fordham's heart had been turned to Mary. Henry was enjoying Fordham's rare show of affection almost as much as Fordham was. What both Henry and Fordham did not realize was that Mary was fulfilling her lifetime dream. The happiness she felt in her little heart could fill the whole inn.

Logan and Johnny had both gone out to help Ethan hook up his sleigh. They both offered to accompany him, but he convinced them he could make the trip quicker alone. Ethan explained that the trail was not suitable for an automobile.

Johnny was relieved that Ethan did not need his help since he was concerned about leaving Molly, even for a few hours. Johnny made it a point to have Ethan include in his telegram to Molly's family that Dr. Allen was available to help Molly if necessary, although she was not expected to deliver for a few days. Johnny knew that Molly's physician father would be relieved with this added assurance. Dr. Allen would not allow any of his guests to reimburse him for sending the telegraph messages.

Logan was likewise glad Ethan did not need his assistance since he was enjoying his discovery of Laura and did not want to miss any precious moments with her.

When Logan and Johnny returned to the drawing room, they found Laura, Molly, Constance, Patience, and Sabrina occupied with one another's company. Millicent and Martha were visiting with each other. Frank was busily engaged in conversation with Fordham and Henry. Little Mary remained seated between the Parsons brothers. A very large smile filled her small face. She enjoyed the moment and the conversation and said nothing. Dr. Allen was busy telling Sam and Sara one of the many stories he had created during his lifetime to entertain his children, grandchildren, and great-grandchildren. Logan and Johnny decided not to disturb the group and opted to take a walk through the small village.

The Bradford Inn was on the edge of the village by the side of the only road leading to and from Ashton. While it was an inn and often was frequented by travelers visiting in Ashton. Dr. Allen also had several rooms of the inn set aside for his medical practice. Dr. Allen's grandfather, Thomas Bradford, built the twenty-four-room inn over forty years prior to the founding of the village. Dr. Allen was born in the inn, and it had remained his residence for his entire life. He had always enjoyed sharing it with others.

Constance Alden also lived at the inn. She had been orphaned when she was seven years old. Dr. Allen, an old family friend, became her legal guardian and surrogate father. Constance was of great help to Millicent and had assisted her and Dr. Allen with the raising of Patience, Sabrina, and Mary, all of whom she referred to as her sisters.

As Logan and Johnny walked through Ashton, they enjoyed the peace and calm. No one else was on the streets. Logan remarked, "What a quaint little village, almost out of a storybook. This town does not belong in the twentieth century. Nothing about it reminds me of any place I've ever been, even here in New England."

Johnny nodded in agreement. "What a peaceful place to reside. It is as though time has stood still here. This village is unblemished from the world I am used to. I envy the people who live here."

Logan added, "Progress has not passed by Ashton. The village has escaped the claws of the twentieth century and has not allowed itself to be deceived. It remains today pure and unblemished by those who would otherwise change it. I would like to imagine that this is the way heaven will be—something to really look forward to."

Johnny added approvingly, "Amen!"

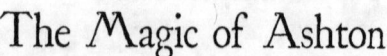

The Magic of Ashton

Lost in time, hidden and removed,
    From the ever-changing world,
The quaint little village of Ashton
    Exists peacefully and quietly.

Escaping the claws, and so-called progress,
    Of the twentieth century,
It stands as a reminder
    Of what has been lost.

It remains today, pure and unblemished,
    By those who would otherwise change it.
Imagine that this wonderful haven
    Is the way heaven will be.

Something to really look forward to!

Journal entry of Logan Emory
March 26, 1970

Chapter Ten

Unselfish Love

Shortly after nine o'clock at night, Johnny and Logan returned to the inn. Everyone was singing Christmas carols, accompanied by Millicent on her piano. This continued until 9:40, when Ethan returned from Waterbury and announced that his trip had been successful. He told everyone that while he was away, he was thinking about Samuel and Sara. A little Christmas song came to his mind. As soon as he could, he wanted to write the words and music down on paper. Ethan picked up his guitar and walked over to where Samuel and Sara were sitting.

Ethan told them, "The Christmas song I composed for both of you is called 'Little Children, Blessed Children.' It goes like this."

Ethan sang the song to the children. It was a fun Christmas song about Santa Claus's forthcoming visit. It concluded with the words, "And Santa Claus will come!"

Samuel and Sara giggled with delight. Ethan noticed the joy that had overcome them. He told everyone, "Many say that Christmas is for children. I believe that Christmas is for everyone. I hope there is still a child in all of us so we can all enjoy the magic of Christmas as much as little children do."

Laura was touched that Ethan would make the effort to compose a special song for her children. The words of the song indicated that Santa Claus would come and leave presents for them. She knew Ethan was unaware that Santa's presents for Samuel and Sara were still at Sullivan's Toy Shop in Boston.

Dr. Allen looked at his pocket watch. "Oh my! How the evening has flown! I fear it is way past bedtime for the children. St. Nicholas won't come if we all stay up.

"Before we all retire, it has been the tradition in this home as far back as I can remember to conclude Christmas Eve with reading in the Gospel according to St. Luke about the glorious birth of Jesus of Nazareth. We are privileged to have in our presence one of New England's most gifted teachers and lecturers. Dr. Fordham Wadsworth Parsons is an esteemed professor emeritus of Harvard University. I would like to invite him to read." With that, Dr. Allen placed the family Bible in Fordham's lap.

Fordham was stunned. He tried to open his mouth to decline. No words could audibly be deciphered. Fordham could not speak or formulate his declination. He looked down at little Mary. Her trusting eyes and face glowed with happiness and excitement. For her, for this dear, sweet child, for this little Mary, he would read the scriptures he so cherished as a child. His mind momentarily raced back in time to when he was a small boy and each Christmas Eve his mother read to him about the heralded birth of the Christ Child. He was caught up in this moment of retrospect.

"Dr. Parsons! Dr. Parsons, are you all right?" Fordham looked up as Dr. Allen was shaking his shoulder gently.

"Yes, yes, I am fine. Just a touch of melancholia." Fordham swallowed hard. His posture was erect as he walked to the hearth. The glow of the flames illuminated his face. His countenance radiated as though an angel had touched him. Little Mary was standing by his side, holding his aged hand with her small, delicate fingers. Dr. Allen's Bible was opened to the Gospel according to St. Luke and was held in a firm grasp in Fordham's right hand. In one swift motion, Fordham placed the Bible on the mantle, and its pages closed. Several seconds passed. A deep smile was on Fordham's face. He recited, from memory of years long past, the words that he had heard many times from his mother's lips.

During Fordham's recitation, all eyes were fixed on him. He spoke with great clarity, firmness, dignity, and eloquence. His distinguished countenance continued to glow. Love radiated from little Mary to Fordham and in turn filled the spacious room.

No one else spoke—not even a whisper. The stage was Fordham's, and he did not disappoint anyone. When he concluded, his eyes were filled with tears of happiness. All the pain of sixty-seven years ago and the years since seemed to dissipate. He was overcome with emotion. He could not speak further and quietly sat down. Henry felt he had just witnessed a miracle. Mary knew she had.

Dr. Allen once again addressed the gathering: "Before we retire, would you all please join me in the dining room? Mary has prepared a special treat for us."

As the group began leaving the drawing room, Dr. Allen briefly detained Fordham and Henry. He especially wanted to thank them for their presence in his home and for Fordham's meaningful recitation. The three men were the last to enter the dining room. Everyone else had taken his or her place at the table. Smiles adorned all of their faces. They began to sing "Happy Birthday" to Henry.

Fordham and Henry were surprised to see a string banner near the far end of the dining room table. It was attached from one wall to the opposite wall. The large letters read, "Happy Birthday, Henry!" A birthday cake with a large, single lighted candle had been placed at the head of the table.

Dr. Allen motioned for Henry to take his place of honor. Moments later, Dr. Allen explained, "Henry, we know you celebrated your birthday earlier today with your brother and friends. We wanted to add our congratulations. Mary baked you a cake. I asked her to place only one candle on it. I learned long ago how difficult it can be to blow out a lot of candles. Mary has also made a special gift for you. It is not quite ready. She will give it to you tomorrow."

Shortly after finishing eating birthday cake, luggage was retrieved from each of the vehicles. Millicent, Constance, and Dr. Allen were all busily showing each of their guests to his or her room. Constance helped Laura get Samuel and Sara ready for bed. Laura was deeply impressed with her. She knew that Constance would make a great mother someday because of the great amount of consideration and love Constance gave to the children. Patience, Sabrina, and Mary also retired to their rooms. All the children would have trouble falling asleep that night. That seems to be the nature of all children on Christmas Eve. As the women were preparing the children for bed, the men were busily bringing in presents from their automobiles.

Logan removed the tag from the gift that he had planned to give to Jan and made a new tag for Laura. He placed the gift carefully under the Christmas tree in the drawing room. He made new tags for other presents, which he had bought for his friends. These gifts would now be given to Johnny and Molly, Ethan and Constance, Dr. Allen and Millicent, Frank and Martha, and Fordham and Henry. He was excited to realize that he also had gifts suitable for Samuel, Sara, Patience, Sabrina, and Mary. He could not have planned it any better.

Henry was also removing old tags on the presents that he had planned to give his family and replaced them with new tags. The presents for grandson Jonah became Samuel's. The presents for granddaughter Mary became Sara's. Gifts meant for his daughter

Louisa would be given to Constance, Martha, Millicent, Molly, and Laura. He marveled that he even had presents that were suitable for Patience, Sabrina, and Mary. He had gone a little overboard this Christmas, he realized. He always wanted to shower his family with Christmas gifts. This was what his late wife did. When she died, Henry continued the practice. He knew Katherine would approve and so would Louisa. Gifts intended for son-in-law Michael were retagged for Dr. Allen, Ethan, Frank, Johnny, and Logan.

After Henry placed all of the presents under the tree, he remembered that there was still one gift left. That one would be given to Fordham. It was the present he had purchased for Fordham several years before, when he hoped he could talk his brother into spending Christmas with him. Fordham, as usual, had declined. From then on, Henry just kept the gift in his suitcase in the event Fordham had a last-minute change of heart. He retrieved the present and placed it under the tree.

Frank and Martha also retagged their presents. The gifts they had for their baby granddaughter would be given to Johnny and Molly for their unborn child. Frank and Martha too were thankful they had so many presents to share with their new friends.

Laura appeared in the drawing room and noticed presents under the tree for Samuel and Sara. Her heart was full. At least there will be some presents under the tree for them, even if Santa could not come. She had tried to prepare her children so they would not be disappointed.

"Santa will come, Mama," Sara had tried to assure her. "I know his reindeer will find us."

If only we could all have the faith little children have, Laura concluded, *everything would be all right.*

Laura wanted to give everyone presents, but there were only two gifts wrapped in her car, one for her father and one for her mother. Laura retagged them and placed them under the tree for Dr. Allen and Millicent. It was Laura's way of thanking them for opening up their home and their hearts to her and the children. Laura especially wanted to give Constance a gift. She had only known this young woman for a few hours, but something about Constance had touched Laura's heart. She was drawn to her and felt a deep amount of love for her. It was hard to explain. At that moment, Laura knew what she would do. She wrapped the dress she had made and worn to worship services that morning. She and Constance were about the same size. This would be her gift to Constance.

Laura knew something special was happening between her and Logan. She was trying to reason how, in less than six hours, her whole world could be changing. It was hard for her to understand how such a prominent man from such a prestigious family could be drawn to her. Her mind reasoned that it was not possible. Her heart sensed that it was. Her heart won. Laura had only one gift that she could give to Logan. Quickly, she wrapped the gift and placed it under the tree for him. She sighed deeply and was not sure if it were relief or fear she was experiencing.

Johnny and Molly also had been retagging the gifts that they had planned to give to Molly's father, stepmother, two brothers, sister-in-law, nieces, and nephews. Johnny and Molly were so happy when they finished placing the presents under the tree. They too marveled that they had enough presents for everyone.

Millicent, along with Ethan and Constance, brought their presents to be placed under the tree. They found there was no room. They placed their gifts behind the tree, along the back wall.

Dr. Allen entered the room. "My, my, my, my, my! There sure are a lot of presents." He stooped and checked a number of tags. "I see there are presents for everyone. I know I will enjoy your gifts to me. I pray that you will enjoy the gift I have for each of you!"

It was nearly eleven o'clock. Dr. Allen and Millicent excused themselves and retired to their rooms. Fordham and Henry soon followed.

Logan and Laura, Johnny and Molly, Ethan and Constance, and Frank and Martha thought the drawing room, in its decorated elegance for the Christmas season, was the ultimate romantic setting. The only light in the room came from the candles on the Christmas tree and the mantle and from the burning logs, which flickered in the fireplace. Constance sat at the piano and began to play "Greensleeves" and other Christmas hymns of an era past. Ethan stood at the piano and sang to Constance's accompaniment.

Logan and Laura felt a mixture of surprise, excitement, and trepidation. Somehow they both knew that they belonged together. They had known each other for only a few hours, yet from the very moment they became acquainted, they both realized that something very special was happening between them. They felt they would never be apart. It was as though it was meant to be—for them to meet, discover each other, and fall in love. The setting could not have been more perfect—the romantic atmosphere of the Bradford Inn in the picturesque village of Ashton at Christmastime. The feelings between them were very strong, and words were not needed. In this setting, they shared their first kiss.

Johnny and Molly were filled with elation as they anticipated the birth of their child.

Ethan and Constance knew that life could not get any better.

Frank and Martha both felt a renewed love for each other and looked forward to a brighter tomorrow.

At midnight, the couples all wished one another a merry Christmas. The candles on the tree and over the hearth were all tapped. The embers of the logs in the fireplace were banked for the night. The only light now present was from the candles on the candleholders that each person held as all retired to their respective rooms. The inn grew dark as each one blew out his or her own candle.

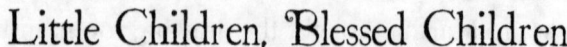

Little Children, Blessed Children

Little children, blessed children,
Full of holiday cheer,
Looking forward to Santa Claus' visit.

Will he bring you? Yes, he'll bring you,
What you asked for this year,
If you've been good boys and girls.

Did you remember? I hope you remembered
To write Santa this year,
So he could bring you a lot of nice presents.

If you didn't, yes, if you didn't
Write to Santa this year,
You will just have to take your chances.

He gets mixed up, just a little mixed up,
If you don't write him each year.
He may not be sure what to bring you.

I can hear Santa. Yes, I hear Santa
Saying to Mrs. Claus this year,
"No letter! No letter, from Sam or Sara!"

Should I leave a doll for Sara? No! I'll leave it for Sam.
That's what I'll do this year.
And I will leave a ball and bat for Sara.

Little children, blessed children,
Full of holiday cheer,
Hoping that Santa won't get mixed up.

Little children, blessed children,
Just remember this year
That is why Santa has elves and reindeer.

They will help him. Yes, they will help him,
To remember this year,
Each present that he should bring you.

Little children, blessed children,
Looking forward this year,
Looking forward to Santa Claus' visit.

Little children, blessed children,
It's now, that time, this year,
To go to bed, so Santa can make his visit!

And, Santa Claus will come!

Ethan

Unselfish Love

Sharing with a stranger,
Stopping to lend a hand,
Walking a mile for another,
Tending to the needs of a neighbor.

Going hungry, so another may eat,
Going without, so another might have.
Donations without compensation,
Offerings without notice or recognition.

Visiting the sick and the elderly,
Giving a lift to the helpless.
Caring for the widows and the fatherless,
Giving lodging to the homeless.

Giving our time to serve the needs of others,
And forgetting our own needs and pleasures.
Being a friend to the friendless,
Tending to the needs of all children.

Forfeiting one's life for family, friend,
Neighbor, God or country.
Serving, ministering, tending, teaching,
And sharing without acclaim.

All examples of unselfish love!

Journal entry of Henry Parsons
November 17, 1916

Chapter Eleven

Early Christmas Morning

Monday, December 25, 1950

Logan heard the knock on his door. His room was still dark. He heard Dr. Allen's voice calling out to him. "Mr. Emory, breakfast will be served at half past the hour. I've left you a kettle of hot water outside your door."

Half past what hour? Logan wondered, still half-asleep. It took a few minutes for him to fully wake up. He was a guest at the Bradford Inn. No electricity! No indoor plumbing! No hot shower! Slowly, everything was coming back to him.

For the next few minutes, Logan reviewed the events of the previous day. A smile crossed his face as he recalled meeting Laura and the evening events that followed. He began to chuckle to himself. For a moment, he thought he dreamed it. Yes, it really did happen! His trip to the outdoor privy in the middle of the night proved that!

Logan had not taken a candle, as there was a full moon and he did not think he would need one. There were two privies behind the Bradford Inn, one for children and one for adults.

The inside of the adult privy was very dark. Logan was familiar with it because he had been there earlier in the evening. At that time, he had a candle with him. It was the largest privy he had ever seen—a four-seater.

Sure is dark in here, Logan thought as he entered the privy. Seconds later, he realized he was not alone.

"Male or female?" a husky voice inquired.

With that, Logan and Johnny Maverick both had a big laugh. Both vowed never to leave their candlesticks behind again and to lock the inside latch of the privy.

Fully awake now, Logan lit his candle. He looked at his pocket watch on the nearby table—six minutes past six. *The sun won't make its appearance for another hour,* he thought. *Why do we have to get up now? It's Christmas morning!* Then he realized he had answered his own question. *Because it's Christmas morning!* His mind wandered back in time to his childhood with his sisters, Nancy Anne and Catherine Mary. He remembered how each Christmas morning they could hardly wait to see what Santa had left them under their Christmas tree.

The hot water felt good on Logan's face. He quickly gave himself a sponge bath. It was not like the early morning shower he was used to. After shaving, grooming, and dressing, Logan drifted out into the hallway. The aroma of bacon and maple syrup hit his nostrils. As he descended the stairs leading to the ground level of the inn, Logan noticed that the double door leading to the drawing room had been padlocked. A deep grin crossed his face. *That must be Santa's way of keeping the children out until breakfast is over*, he concluded and chuckled to himself.

Logan entered the dining room. He was the first guest to arrive. Millicent and her girls were all in the kitchen, putting the finishing touches on breakfast. Logan noticed the dining room clock... 6:24. There was enough time for a quick trip to the privy, he decided. Grabbing a candle, he exited through the rear door of the inn.

Hearing the voices of Dr. Allen and Ethan in the barn nearby, Logan went to investigate. Witnessing the birth of a calf, he smiled and remarked, "Not Baby Jesus, but totally appropriate for Christmas."

"The birthing process respects no holidays," laughed Dr. Allen.

When Logan returned to the dining room, everyone was seated except for the servers, and Dr. Allen and Ethan, who were still out in the barn. Laura had saved the seat next to her for Logan. As she smiled at him, a warm feeling went through his body. He sat down next to Laura, and she placed her hand gently on his arm. His hand quickly found hers, and she moved a little closer to him. The feeling of love between them was so intense that Logan wondered if the others could feel it also.

Logan thought about a future with Laura. He knew that he did not want to spend another day without her. Being together for the rest of their lives seemed so right and so natural. Together forever! He knew from her gentle touch and from the way she looked at him that she felt the same. *So this is what it feels like to really fall in love.* It was such an exhilarating and wonderful experience.

Logan told everyone about the arrival of the baby calf. It was all he could do to restrain Samuel and Sara from investigating.

Millicent quietly slipped out the rear door of the inn as her girls were placing bowls of fruit, hot cereals, scrambled eggs, potatoes, gravies, and hotcakes; covered baskets of biscuits, rolls, and muffins; and plates of sliced ham, bacon, and steak on the table. There was also plenty of hot maple syrup and fresh homemade butter, jellies, and preserves of every kind. The guests marveled at the great display of food.

"My diet starts tomorrow," said Frank jokingly.

Laughter erupted throughout the room.

As quietly as she left, Millicent returned. The guests were

chatting among themselves and did not notice her appear at the entrance of the dining room. She struck the dinner bell several times to gain everyone's attention and then announced, "Dr. Allen and Ethan will be joining us shortly. It is the tradition in this household that Dr. Allen always sits at the head of this table and pronounces the blessing on the food. It is his belief that when a family eats together and prays together, they will always remain together. This Christmas morning, breakfast will be delayed a few minutes. There have been times when we have waited hours for my father."

"One night, we all missed supper because Papa never came home until the next morning," Patience related.

"A very difficult delivery." Millicent added.

Laughter filled the room again.

At precisely 6:50, Dr. Allen and Ethan took their places at the table. After offering apologies, Dr. Allen asked Millicent for the family Bible. "This morning I would like to read the first chapter of the first book of the Holy Bible." When Dr. Allen concluded reading, he asked everyone to hold hands and join him in reciting the Lord's Prayer. Dr. Allen added his thanks for his home, his family's blessings, the presence of his visitors and their families, and for the birth, life, and ministry of Jesus Christ. He ended by blessing the food and all of the hands that prepared it.

Little Sara figured out that Dr. Allen had blessed about everything there was to bless. As Dr. Allen said, "Amen," Samuel questioned politely, "Now can we eat?" Smiles adorned everyone's faces.

"Yes, my child, let's all eat," answered Dr. Allen, trying not to laugh.

As the food was being passed around the table, the host of the inn explained why his family served only milk, homemade berry juices, and peppermint and other homemade teas. "In this home, we eat only what we grow or raise or what I receive in-kind for my professional services. We avoid anything that I, as a physician, know to be harmful to our bodies."

None of the guests were offended. How could they be? The generosity of Dr. Bradford Allen and his family was overwhelming. All the guests felt so welcomed in his home that it was as though they all belonged there. It was as if they were part of Dr. Allen's family. They were all total strangers to one another. In the fourteen hours since they had been together, the love and kinship they felt for one another was something they could not comprehend. They felt safe, warm, and loved. The day was just beginning.

After everyone finished eating, all the women, except Molly, cleared the dining table and tended to the chores of the kitchen. Dr. Allen asked Molly, Samuel, and Sara to join him in his office so he could entertain them with one of his favorite stories. This morning, he chose his own expanded version of Dr. Clement Moore's *A Visit from St. Nicholas*.

Logan and Johnny joined Ethan as he tended to his cow and her newborn calf. Ethan explained that his day began each morning at four. He would milk the cows and feed and tend to the needs of the cattle, horses, mules, pigs, and chickens on the Allen farm. Logan joked that his day was not much different as he often arose early to study trial briefs and do legal research in his vast personal law library.

Frank, Fordham, and Henry were visiting together as they sat in the tall, deep, leather-bound chairs that graced the wide hallway of the inn. At precisely eight o'clock, Dr. Allen gathered everyone into the hallway. He announced that everyone would enter the drawing room together, with the children going first, followed by the adults. He joked that he and Fordham would bring up the rear.

Dr. Allen unlocked the padlock on the drawing room doors. All could see the eagerness of little Samuel and Sara. Laura's heart dropped. In all of the excitement of the morning, she had forgotten that the presents they hoped Santa would bring would not be there—thanks only to Mr. Fitzgerald!

What Laura and the other guests saw next was almost indescribable. Gasps filled the room. The drawing room seemed to have been transformed overnight into the most beautiful and elegant Christmas room any one of them had ever beheld. It was the same Christmas tree and the same presents under the tree as the night before. The furniture was the same, and nothing seemed to have been moved. There was a warm glow in the room. The sun had been up for nearly an hour, and natural light flooded the room. The snow-covered ground of the countryside, seen through the windows that filled the outer wall, added to the warmth and elegance of the room.

Christmas flowers of every kind filled large vases throughout the room. It was a perplexing moment for Martha Masters, past president of the Lowell Garden Club. Where did Dr. Allen get all these flowers, most of which were foreign to New England, especially in December?

It was as though Dr. Allen could read her mind. "St. Nicholas," Dr. Allen proudly proclaimed. "He delivered them when he brought the toys."

Laura's heart was full. She felt as though she were in the middle of a dream. She could not believe her eyes! However, she was even more shocked when she noticed all of the toys she had laid away at Sullivan's Toy Shop back in Boston. They were now all laid out under the Christmas tree here at the Bradford Inn. How could this be?

Laura felt Dr. Allen's gentle touch on her shoulder as he pulled her to him and whispered quietly into her ear. "St. Nicholas, Father Christmas, Santa Claus—whatever you choose to call him—he delivered them while you were asleep."

Gratitude filled Laura's heart, and her eyes began to tear. She turned, hugged Dr. Allen, and kissed his cheek. "You dear, dear man. Oh, you wonderful man! I don't know how you did it or even why. I just know that I believe in Santa Claus. I wonder if maybe you could be Santa Claus!"

In addition, to the toys for Samuel and Sara, there were beautiful porcelain dolls and other gifts for Patience, Sabrina, and Mary. The adults witnessed the excitement displayed by the children as they discovered the gifts that Santa had left for each of them. Then Dr. Allen drew everyone's attention to the long mantle. There was a stocking for everyone, even the unborn child of Johnny and Molly.

The person who enjoyed his stocking the most was Dr. Fordham Parsons. The stockings were filled with homemade candies, nuts, and caramel popcorn balls.

The stocking of the unborn baby was filled with rattles, blocks, and other small toys that an infant would enjoy. The toys were special for Johnny and Molly. The silver-plated rattles were inscribed: "Col. Aaron Buck, silversmith, Ashton, Vermont." The wooden toys were of the finest craftsmanship, and Johnny and Molly suspected that they too were crafted in Ashton.

The men all found a very special gift at the bottom of each of their stockings: a finely crafted wooden top and a string to spin it with.

"It's been over sixty years," Fordham chuckled, "but I'm game."

"Not on my hardwood floors!" exclaimed a frightened Millicent.

Dr. Allen came to his daughter's rescue. "There is a place out back by the barn that is good for spinning tops. After we have opened the gifts, the boys—I mean, the men—can all go out and spin their tops."

"And play with our marbles too!" exclaimed an excited fifty-two-year-old Frank Masters.

Santa had also left a bag of marbles at the very bottom of each of the men's stockings. Samuel also received a top and bag of marbles in his stocking.

At the bottom of each of the stockings for the women and girls, including Sara, was an exquisite silver locket. Each locket contained a small oval picture of Dr. Allen and a small oval portrait of a woman. Laura and the others knew the woman was Temperance, Dr. Allen's first wife, since her portrait hung in the drawing room. Millicent had previously explained to the guests that the painting was a portrait of her mother. Laura wondered why Dr. Allen had not just placed an actual photo of Temperance in the locket as he had of himself. She concluded that he favored the portrait. The locket for Patience contained photographs of her father and of her mother, Jane.

Also in each of the women's stockings was a silver-plated comb and brush set of the finest craftsmanship. As with the silver-plated rattles, each set was inscribed with, "Col. Aaron Buck, silversmith, Ashton, Vermont." These were special gifts. Laura, Molly, and Martha together concluded that Santa really did exist, and his alias was Dr. Bradford Allen, physician, innkeeper, and farmer of Ashton, Vermont.

Never in any of their lives had the guests met anyone like Dr. Allen. They all felt a very special love for him—a love they could not understand or explain.

I Believe in Santa Claus

Adorned with lights and ornaments of every color,
    Wrapped presents beneath its branches,
The Christmas tree was beautiful. Rays of light
    Glistened from the silver star on the top.

Festive decorations, wreaths, poinsettias,
    Holly and mistletoe!
Toys set out, stockings filled,
    Evidence that Santa had been there.

Anticipation, excited hearts of children,
    Young and old alike.
I wonder what is in that big box,
    And in that small one too?

Please, believe in Santa Claus,
    Even if he missed your house.
Perhaps he was sick a week or two.
    And did not get all the presents made.

I remember the year that Dad was out of work,
    And we could not afford a tree.
I know that Santa still came,
    Even though he did not leave us any toys.

He knew there were other things we needed more:
    Warm coats and shoes for our feet.
A basket of food he left at our front door,
    And a note that said our rent had been paid.

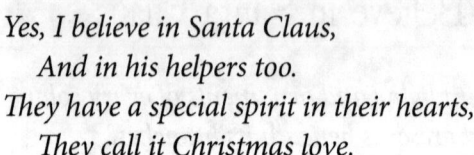

Yes, I believe in Santa Claus,
And in his helpers too.
They have a special spirit in their hearts,
They call it Christmas love.

Or, should we say Christlike love?

Journal entry of William Henry Brewster
June 7, 1957

Chapter Twelve

Gifts of Love

Dr. Allen began passing out the Christmas gifts. As each one was opened, each recipient expressed astonishment and thankfulness. The presents seemed to be tailored exactly to their needs, size, color and desire. Each gift was very special. Had they not known any better, they would have thought it was purchased especially for them.

When Laura received her gift from Logan, she could not believe her eyes. It was the most beautiful diamond ring she had ever seen. She looked into his searching eyes. "This was meant for someone else?" she questioned.

"No! It was meant for the woman I will marry!" Logan said emphatically. "It wasn't the ring that I had originally planned to give Jan, the one she selected and had sized. When I went to pick it up, this ring caught my eye and I was drawn to it. I felt impressed to leave the other ring with the jeweler. There was no time to have it sized. This ring was meant for you. I would be honored if you would consent to be my wife." Logan looked pleadingly into Laura's eyes.

"Yes! Yes! Yes!" was all that Laura could say, as tears of joy filled her eyes.

When Logan slipped the ring on Laura's finger, it was a perfect fit.

Laura asked Dr. Allen to retrieve the gift she had for Logan. Logan very carefully unwrapped it. It was a sterling silver chain necklace with a small silver-plated heart. The inscription on it read, "Laura Ann 3-3-22". Laura explained, "Logan, my father gave this to me on the day I was born. It is symbolic of my heart and of my love for you. It is the only gift I have to give to you."

Logan took Laura in his arms and gently kissed her lips. "Laura, this is the greatest gift you could ever give me, since it comes from your heart. You are wrong when you say it is the only gift you have for me today. Loving me and consenting to be my wife was the first gift. Allowing me to be a father to Sam and Sara was the second. This necklace is the third. I have never received three more meaningful gifts."

Dr. Allen quickly surveyed the room. Millicent and several of the others were weeping. Sam and Sara were excited, although they were not really sure what all of this meant. Everyone congratulated the happy couple.

Dr. Allen allowed the moment to continue, but then became a bit impatient and exclaimed, "There are more presents to open!"

Ethan gave Johnny and Molly an exquisite crib, which he said he crafted especially for their baby. They marveled at its fine craftsmanship and inlaid wood marquetry. They exclaimed that it must have taken him days to complete the intricate artwork, sanding and staining.

"Two whole weeks!" exclaimed an excited Constance.

Johnny and Molly both realized that the crib was actually meant for Ethan and Constance's children, but they were willing to allow themselves to believe that Ethan had really crafted it for their child. They had only known him for a few hours. This gift was created with his own hands and with all of his heart. It was, and would always be, a most cherished gift.

Constance, Sabrina, Patience and Mary brought their gifts to Johnny and Molly. They had knitted a large blanket for the baby and, also, had made a beautiful comforter and several other blankets with intricate sewing and needlework. They had knitted a Sunday outfit with booties to match and had sewn several other outfits for the baby. There was, also, a large supply of handmade diapers. Molly knew that it had taken a lot of time to create these beautiful gifts. She and Johnny felt a deeper love for each of them. The same kind of love they felt for Ethan.

Millicent retrieved five large packages and gave one each to Fordham, Henry, Johnny and Molly, Logan and Laura, and the last to Frank and Martha. Each one contained a very large quilt—the kind that took quilting bees weeks to make. Each was different and seemed to tell a different story. They seemed to have been made with the recipient in mind. They each knew this was not possible, but the impossible had been happening over and over again, ever since they came to Ashton, less than eighteen hours ago.

Constance excitedly added, "Ethan and I were given our quilt on the day that Papa Allen announced our betrothal."

Martha, Molly and Laura hugged Millicent and could not stop crying tears of happiness. The men were all totally stunned and speechless. Who was this wonderful, unselfish woman, who had an abundance of love for these total strangers?

Dr. Allen allowed this moment to continue and then announced that there were more presents to open.

Constance, Sabrina, Patience and Mary retrieved a long box about six feet long, two and a half feet wide, and two feet deep. The wrapping paper was handmade, as it was on all of the presents given to the guests by Dr. Allen's family. The elegant ribbon and very large bow was also handmade. The package was so stunningly beautiful, that Logan and Laura were reluctant to open it when it was given to them. They carefully unwrapped the gift, and as they viewed its contents, tears of gratitude and happiness filled Laura's eyes. Inside the box was the most beautiful wedding dress that she had ever seen. Thousands of beads were sewn onto the dress and its extremely long train. Laura knew that months of tedious needlework went into the creation of this grandest and most beautiful of all wedding dresses.

"Constance, this is your wedding dress, isn't it?" questioned Laura. "I cannot accept it."

"Constance answered, "No, Laura, the girls and I made this dress especially for you. Grandmother Millicent is making mine."

"How could all of you have known?" questioned Logan. "I just asked Laura to marry me." Yet, the card accompanying the gift read, "To Laura and Logan, with love from Constance, Sabrina, Patience and Mary".

When Ethan brought his gift to Logan and Laura, one could have heard a pin drop. All eyes focused on them to note their reaction. The card read, "To Logan and Laura, cordially, Ethan".

The whole room erupted in laughter when another crib appeared. Logan and Laura tearfully hugged Ethan and thanked him for this precious gift.

Frank remarked, "That is one present that I know Martha and I are not going to receive."

Laughter, again, filled the room.

Ethan retrieved a large present, two feet by three feet and six inches deep. "This gift is to Frank and Martha from Mary. She has a special talent," Ethan explained.

"Ethan helped me," added Mary.

"Hush, Mary, before you spoil the surprise!" warned Ethan.

"The paper is so pretty and the bow is so elegant," exclaimed a thrilled Martha. "I hate to open it."

After Frank and Martha opened the present, they, very carefully, lifted a large portrait from inside. Their eyes opened wider as they beheld the faintingly familiar images that gazed at them from within the portrait. It took a moment for them to realize who the couple in the portrait was, but when they did, they were speechless. They could not ask for an explanation. Tears flowed from their eyes.

Ethan explained, "Your twins would be twenty years old now, had they lived. Mary has painted their portraits together as they might appear today, if you were allowed to see them in heaven. Mary asked me to make the frame, but the gift is from her and comes from deep within her heart."

Frank and Martha knew that they were in Ashton, Vermont. But, as far as they were concerned, Ashton was heaven. The portrait, which they were viewing, was that of the two young carolers, on whom their eyes had been fixed the previous evening. Logically they knew they were really not their children. But logic no longer existed for any of the guests at the Bradford Inn on Christmas Day 1950. All Frank and Martha could do was to hold this little angel, Mary, in their arms and weep tears of joy and gratitude.

Ethan retrieved another large present similar in size to the one given to Frank and Martha. He placed it on the floor in front of Fordham and Henry, who were seated on a sofa with little Mary. She had reclaimed her favorite place, wedged in between them.

Ethan explained, "This very special gift is from Mary. It is also a gift from her heart to yours. I know that it will be a gift that you both will cherish for the rest of your lives. Your family will, also, cherish it for generations to come."

Fordham and Henry's hands trembled as they very carefully removed the handmade ribbon and wrapping paper. As they lifted a large painted portrait from the box, also encased in one of Ethan's exquisite handcrafted frames, Fordham paused, and then exclaimed, "It's a portrait of our mother! She died when I was ten years old. How can this be? My father was so heartbroken that he destroyed all of her pictures. I have not looked upon her beautiful face for sixty-seven years, but I know the woman in this portrait is my mother. Her face is etched upon my memory."

Henry could only stare at the portrait. His mother died giving birth to him. He had never known what she looked like. The portrait depicted a very beautiful woman, who appeared to be in her mid-thirties. His feeling was one of total elation.

Ethan produced another large present and placed it in front of Henry. Ethan explained, "This is your birthday present from Mary."

Fordham helped his brother open the gift. The box contained another large hand-painted portrait. It was a family portrait of them, with both of their parents, as they all would have appeared when Henry was about ten years old, if their mother had lived.

With their family, in the portrait, was a young lady who appeared to be in her late twenties. Fordham and Henry were speechless. They both understood the significance of this family portrait. The young lady strongly resembled their mother. Anyone looking at the portrait would assume they were mother and daughter. Their features were nearly identical.

Fordham and Henry both felt a strong impression that the young lady was their older sister, the sister they never knew. They had reason to previously suspect her existence, but until now, they had no sure evidence of it.

Fordham had revealed sometime ago, his strong feeling of the existence of an older sister. This occurred after Henry had finished reading their father's journals. Henry had noticed, several references to their mother's "pain that she always carried with her". Their father never identified this "pain". Henry had asked Fordham if he knew what was meant by this "pain" with which their mother had been plagued.

Fordham explained, "Father never answered any of my questions concerning Mother. My knowledge of her exists only from my own memory. I know nothing of her life before she went to work for Father. However, I do have a memory from my early childhood. I was perhaps six years old. I awoke in the middle of the night and heard my mother crying. Father was trying to comfort her. They did not hear me enter their room. I recall hearing Mother say, 'I miss my baby! Will she ever forgive me? Will God forgive me!' I cannot recall what happened after that. I must have gone back to my bed. I never discussed this with Mother. I am not sure that it really did happen. It could have been a dream. It seemed real, and it is and always has been very clear in my mind. Father refused to confirm the existence of the daughter that Mother spoke of and wept over. Knowing Father, if she had never existed, he would have told me. I do not know if the baby died or if Mother had to give her up for adoption. I do not know if Mother had ever been married before. However, I do know the child was not Father's!"

The family portrait was of their entire family, together, as it should have been, except for the tragic loss of their mother and, for whatever reason there was, for her not being able to raise her daughter. Fordham and Henry realized that they were indeed a complete family, and they had always been a complete family, even though, they had not had the opportunity to live together as a family.

What amazed Fordham most, were the faces of Henry, their father and himself. No previous photographer's or artist's brush had ever captured on film, or canvas, what little Mary had been able to do. Their facial expressions and true likeness had never been more accurate than these depicted on this canvas. Mary seemed to have painted them, not through the eyes of an artist, but from the heart of one who knew them like no other. It seemed impossible that little Mary would have been able to do this, unless she had painted through the eyes of inspiration. Oh, how blind are the eyes of many artists!

Tears flowed, unashamedly, from Henry and Fordham's eyes. They sat stone-faced and stunned. All they could do was weep and hug little Mary, whose own eyes were brimming over with tears. Both knew that they could not explain this, or any of the events of the last eighteen hours, to any of their colleagues. They were learned men, who had held positions of great professional responsibility. Their intelligence and credibility had never been questioned. They could not explain all that they had witnessed. They only knew their hearts were full. Had their lives ended at that very moment, they would have left their mortal existence totally contented. They both were speechless and unable to ask Mary the nature of her special talent. The knew she was inspired, and that if an angel really did exist, it existed in the form of their little Mary. They knew she possessed greater gifts, from God, than her ability to paint portraits.

Fordham was a happy man, free now from the chains that had previously held him bondage each Christmas since his mother's death. On this Christmas Day, in 1950, he was filled with complete peace.

Fordham fought hard to say what Henry could not. "Henry, thanks you, Mary. We both thank you. Words cannot express how much this means to both of us." Mary's face beamed with delight.

The others in the room were deeply touched by Mary's gifts to Fordham and Henry. None were affected more than Martha, who turned to her Frank and said quietly to him, "I have a feeling of total peace and elation. Little Mary has brought so much happiness through her paintings."

Martha and Frank did not share with the others what they both, now, knew in their hearts to be true.

Millicent handed a package to Sara. When the child opened it, she beheld an antique doll with a porcelain face. Millicent explained, "Sara, this doll was given to me when I was about your age. Her name is Maggie, and she always was my favorite doll. It is time she found a new home, and I would like her to live with you."

Sara was excited with her doll and gave Millicent a big hug.

Ethan retrieved the presents he had for Sam and Sara. "I don't wrap presents very well," he explained. Then he produced a large sack with a blue bow that he gave to Sam, and a smaller sack with a red bow that he gave to Sara.

Sam was excited as he pulled a beautiful sled out of his sack. Sara pulled a small cradle out of hers. It was exactly the size for the doll that she had just received. Ethan had spent many hours crafting these gifts.

Next, Millicent presented Sam and Sara with sweaters that she had knitted. They fit perfectly, and it was as though the sweaters had been knitted with each of them in mind.

Sara opened a large present from Constance, Sabrina, Patience and Mary. They had made doll clothing for her new doll. She was so excited that she gave each of them a big hug.

Dr. Allen gave a large bag of candy to Sam. He explained that he learned a long time ago, that this was what little boys liked most.

Dr. Allen asked Sabrina, Patience, Mary and Sara to come to his side. "I have something very special for each of you." He produced four small gifts, all the same size. The girls opened their gifts and found that they had each been given identical music boxes. Dr. Allen cautioned them not to open the music boxes, until he instructed, and that they all open them at precisely the same instant. When they did, the most beautiful music filled the air.

Molly's attention was drawn to the music. It was the same tune that came from a music box that her Aunt Patty had given her, when Molly was a small child. It had always been her greatest treasure and her most prized possession.

Aunt Patty had helped raise Molly after her mother's death, which occurred when Molly was still an infant. Her beloved Aunt Patty, also, raised Molly's mother. Molly was thrilled that the girls were getting music boxes with the same music she had always loved. When Patience showed Molly her new music box, a feeling of warmth flowed through Molly's body. She sat stunned and motionless. It looked exactly like the one she had at home. The one that Aunt Patty had given her many years before.

Fordham requested that Ethan come to his side. He, very carefully, removed his pocket watch and the gold chain that went with it. He placed it in the palm of Ethan's hand. "I noticed that you don't have a pocket watch," he explained. "Every man needs a good watch. This one was my father's. It served him well, and has also served me well. I don't have a son to pass it on to. I would like to give it to you as a token of my appreciation and affection. If I had ever been blessed with a son, I would only hope that he would have been as fine a man as I know you to be."

Henry was witnessing another miracle. He knew his brother well. His brother's life had been centered totally around higher academic learning and only on a university level. He had only respected his students, and his peers, who had risen to the very top of their scholastic and professional expertise. He was rendering this great amount of praise on Ethan, who, undoubtedly, only had a simple education. Ethan would likely spend the rest of his life in manual labor.

The remaining gifts under the tree were handed out, and thank-yous were exchanged. Tears flowed freely from everyone's eyes.

For the last hour, Dr. Bradford Allen had been sitting in his favorite chair observing his family and their guests enjoying each other's generosity. A verse in the Bible came to his mind:

> *"This is my commandment,*
> *that ye love one another,*
> *as I have loved you."*
> **John 15:12**

The smile that had been on his face became even more pronounced. He continued to enjoy the moment. It was as though music filled the room and drowned out the chatter of its occupants. Only feelings of complete joy, happiness and love were present and felt by all.

This was the happiest day of Dr. Bradford Allen's life. He had lived a long life, and had known a lot of joy, and had, also, endured a lot of heartache and sorrow. He had always been pleased with his family, but nothing could surpass the love he felt for them now. He was filled with complete peace and joy for the first time in a long while.

Dr. Allen arose slowly from his chair and walked over to the windows. He had always enjoyed the drawing room and the windows that completely filled its outer wall. One could survey the complete countryside and see for several miles. Only the mountains prevented a person from seeing further. Snow covered the ground and the mountains. The view was especially breathtaking.

As his family and guests continued to enjoy themselves, Dr. Allen moved to the hearth and stoked the fire. He added several more logs. This movement focused everyone's attention toward him. Dr. Allen surveyed all their faces. Unspoken words came from their hearts. The room was filled with love.

Dr. Allen swallowed hard, and said, "Last Christmas, Ethan presented me with a very special gift, a poem he had written for me. Ever since Ethan was a small child he, had heard me constantly talk about my wish that everybody throughout the world could feel only love for each other, and that there would be peace everywhere. I would like to share with you Ethan's poem entitled…"

My Christmas Wish

If I had but one wish at this Christmas time,
It would be for peace throughout the world.
That all nations and all mankind would strive to live,
In total harmony with each other, forever.

That wars and rumors of war would cease to exist.
That the lamb and the lion could lie down together.
That the mighty and strong would lay down their weapons.
That fear and destruction be replaced with hope and charity.

One and all working, never idle.
Greed, hatred, envy, lust and poverty would cease to exist.
Everyone sharing and serving each other.
Love, only love, everywhere.

All children growing, never starving,
Looking forward to tomorrow.
If I had but one wish at this Christmas time,
It would be that peace and love would reign everywhere.

Dr. Allen paused for a few moments and said, "If everyone in the world could feel the love that is present in this room today, I believe mine and Ethan's wish could come true." A deep smile graced his face, and he proceeded to say: "We have all been richly blessed this day. Well, it sure looks pleasant outside. Let's all go for a sleigh ride."

Gifts of Love

After his long work day was finished,
  Fatigued and weary worn,
The young man toiled many days,
  Late into each night.
Carefully chosen, the wood selected
  Was of the finest quality.
With heartfelt purpose,
  With steady and skillful hands,
Patiently, he worked with the wood.
  And when completed,
Cribs for precious babies!
  Gifts created with love!

Four hearts filled with love,
  Eight young delicate hands,
United in purpose
  And dedicated to their task.
Hour after hour, day after day,
  Week after week, month after month,
No one complaining, fingers working,
  Never stopping, steadily sewing
The grandest and most beautiful
  Of all wedding dresses,
For a very special bride!
  A gift created with love!

She had lived many years
  And had known much heartache and pain.

Her life had never been one of ease.
    Her burden had never been light.
Yet, love radiated from within her.
    She never had a cross word for another.
Her caring heart knew no boundaries.
    Service to others was her mission.
Beautiful quilts she made for loved ones.
    They each had a story to tell.
Each made for the recipient!
    Each, a gift created with love!

Chosing a gift for one,
    But giving it to another.
How can that be?
    Have you ever done that before?
A sweater, a tie, or perhaps a toy?
    A puzzle or a piece of jewelry?
The gift given and upon reflection,
    Did you come to realize,
That the gift chosen for another,
    Was given to the right person?
What matters most,
    Is that it was given with love!

A rock from a child's collection,
    A sports card bent and worn with age,
A child's handmade gift, crudely created,
    But made with love.
A meaningful locket or necklace,
    A pocket watch, a favorite book,

All very special and meaningful gifts,
When given from the heart.
Money does not make the gift!
One that is given in love!

Many have talents of which they may be unaware,
Or have chosen to hide.
Have you ever tried to write a poem,
For a loved one or a special friend?
Have you attempted to paint a portrait?
Or draw a sketch of someone you love?
They say the artist's brush is magic,
When its strokes are done in love.
Have you ever tried to write a song?
Or pen a tribute to a friend?
You may be surprised to find,
That you have created a most treasured gift!

All gifts are special that come from the heart!
All are gifts of love!

Journal entry of Logan Emory
June 24, 1996

Chapter Thirteen

Christmas Joy

Johnny and Logan helped Ethan hook up the horses to two big sleighs belonging to the inn. The sleighs were quickly filled. Johnny was not sure that Molly was up for the sleigh ride, but she insisted that she would be all right. Ethan led the group through the streets of Ashton and the surrounding countryside. The snow glistened from the bright sun directly overhead in the clear blue sky. This was quite a contrast from the weather the day before.

It was noon in Ashton, and the streets were filled with sleighs and merrymakers. Families were making snowmen in their yards. The hills of Ashton were filled with young and old enjoying their sleds.

When the Allen family and their guests returned to the inn, everyone enjoyed hot chocolate, cider, rolls, scones, muffins, and sandwiches. Sam decided to try out his new sled and quickly joined other children on a hill nearby. The men stepped outside and tried out their tops and played several games of marbles. Dr. Allen helped Sabrina, Patience, Mary, and Sara build a large snowman in the front yard. The women enjoyed one another's company in the drawing room. Millicent slipped into the kitchen to prepare the evening meal.

Later, Martha, Laura, and Constance stepped outside and began building an arsenal of snowballs. The girls quickly joined them. As the snowballs began flying in the direction of the men, Fordham and Henry retreated to the sidelines with Dr. Allen and Molly. They laughed as they watched the women and girls overpower Frank, Logan, Johnny, and Ethan in a very lopsided snowball fight.

"Not fair," laughed Frank after the men had given up. "You didn't give us a chance."

Everyone was covered with snow, laughing and enjoying the moment.

"Oh no!" yelled Molly. She looked at Dr. Allen and said, "I believe the baby wants to join in on all the fun!"

Johnny quickly picked up Molly and carried her into the inn. Dr. Allen, Millicent, and Constance made preparations for the birth that would soon follow. Everyone else retired nervously to the drawing room.

Several hours later, those in the inn heard the crying of a newborn baby. After a few moments, Dr. Allen appeared at the entrance of the drawing room and announced, "It's a boy!"

At dinner that evening, Johnny told everyone that he and Molly had decided to name their son Bradford Allen Maverick, after the doctor who delivered him.

Dr. Allen laughed as he informed his guests that the most popular male names in Ashton were Bradford and Allen.

After dinner, Johnny excused himself to spend the remainder of the evening with his wife and newborn son. While the women were in the kitchen finishing the dinner chores, Logan and Ethan tended to the animals in the barn. Samuel and Sara cornered Dr. Allen in his office. He surrendered to their desire to hear another one of his many yarns. Frank, Fordham, and

Henry were grateful for the tranquility of the drawing room.

Later, Logan slipped out to his automobile and listened to the Montpelier station on his radio for news on the current road conditions. He learned that the road and power company crews had nearly completed their work on Routes 2 and 100. The roads were expected to be totally cleared and safe for travel by noon the next day.

That evening, the occupants and guests of the Bradford Inn went caroling throughout the village and mingled among the residents. Frank and Martha did not see the two young people to whom they were drawn on Christmas Eve. They had logically concluded that Mary had used them as models for her portraits of Franklin and Frances. Frank and Martha believed that Mary was inspired to sketch their twins as they really would have looked had they still been living.

The remainder of the evening was spent visiting and singing Christmas carols. Millicent accompanied the singing on the piano. She explained that the piano was an old spinet made in Boston in 1848. Everyone marveled that it was still in such immaculate condition.

Ethan appeared with his guitar and treated the guests to another Christmas song he had composed. The words of the song seemed to have been written especially for them. Ethan was blessed with a rich baritone voice. When he concluded his song, he quietly set his guitar aside and recited a poem that he also had written. The words and music touched the hearts of the guests. Fordham realized that he was in the presence of a talented poet and composer.

Fordham spoke, "Ethan, had my foster grandfather been with us this evening, he would have feasted on your beautiful words.

"My earliest childhood memory was Christmas 1876, when I was not yet four years old. My parents were entertaining family and close friends. I was sitting at the feet of my foster grandfather. That was a favorite place of mine.

"Grandfather's lips began to move from within his beautiful, white beard. He was reciting a poem he had written in 1863, during the Civil War. I came to love that poem nearly as much as I loved him. It was my mother's favorite poem. Grandfather recited it for her every Christmas. He was our neighbor and was very fond of my parents. They were married in his home. He loved my mother as though she were his own daughter. He was the only grandfather I ever knew.

"Grandfather died the year before my mother, just a few days after I turned nine years old. When they both had died, the poem, for me, died with them—but not for the world. The poem was set to music and became a favorite Christmas carol. I pray that everyone will indulge me as I recite 'Christmas Bells' by my foster grandfather, Henry Wadsworth Longfellow."

Fordham arose from where he had been seated and began to recite the words that he had so loved as a child.

Christmas Bells

I heard the bells on Christmas Day
Their old, familiar carols play,
And wild and sweet
The words repeat
Of peace on earth, good-will to men!

And thought how, as the day had come,
The belfries of all Christendom
Had rolled along
The unbroken song
Of peace on earth, good-will to men!

Till, ringing, singing on its way,
The world revolved from night to day,

A voice, a chime,
A chant sublime
Of peace on earth, good-will to men!

Then from each black, accursed mouth
The cannon thundered in the South,
*   And with the sound*
*   The carols drowned*
Of peace on earth, good-will to men!

It was as if an earthquake rent
The hearth-stones of a continent,
*   And made forlorn*
*   The households born*
Of peace on earth, good-will to men!

And in despair I bowed my head;
"There is no peace on earth," I said;
*   "For hate is strong,*
*   And mocks the song*
Of peace on earth, good-will to men!"

Then pealed the bells more loud and deep:
"God is not dead; nor doth he sleep!
*   The Wrong shall fail,*
*   The Right prevail,*
With peace on earth, good-will to men!"

As everyone was listening to the poem, one by one, they began to recognize it as the carol "I Heard the Bells on Christmas Day." When Fordham finished his recitation, everyone began to sing what was already a favorite carol for many.

Logan and Laura had known each other for only thirty hours, yet they were both at peace with their decision to be married.

In a private moment, they shared with each other their mutual feeling that they were the last two pieces of a puzzle that was almost complete. It was as though the two pieces had been left behind with the manufacturer of the puzzle. Years had passed, and the puzzle remained incomplete and undisturbed. Then yesterday, without any warning or explanation, the two missing pieces reunited to make the puzzle complete.

As Logan and Laura were sharing their innermost thoughts and feelings, Ethan, Constance, Frank, and Martha joined them and suggested that they all go on a romantic sleigh ride. The heartache Laura felt just thirty hours ago was long gone. Her countenance radiated with her newfound happiness.

There was a full moon. The night air was cold but not harsh. As the sleigh traveled through the countryside, Laura had Logan's strong arm around her. She enjoyed being next to him. She felt safe. Complete peace and pure joy came to her from knowing that she was loved again.

Ethan's Song

There is no place I would rather be on this Christmas day,
　　Than at home with my friends, and my loved ones.
With a cozy fire, homemade candies and holiday treats
　　A Christmas tree, stockings, holly and mistletoe.

Sharing presents, gifts of love, we have opened this day.
　　We have hugged, and we have laughed as friends and loved ones.
Christmas dinner, with all the trimmings, shared
　　With all of you; was even more special than ever.

Tears of joy we have cried, throughout this holiday,
　　As we have enjoyed this time as friends and loved ones.
Singing carols, spending the day in holiday play,
　　Building memories that we will all cherish forever.

There is no place I would rather be on this Christmas day
　　Than at home with my friends, and my loved ones.
There is no place I would rather be in all the days to come
　　Than at home with every one of you—my loved ones!

Ethan

Ethan's Poem

Christmas comes but once a year,
*   The Lord uses carolers and givers to spread His cheer.*
It is a special time we can be with our family,
*   Our friends, and to enjoy each other's company.*
It is a time of reflection, especially for me.
*   Of the gifts my Father has given to me.*

On bended knees, I sincerely pray
*   Thanking my Father for each and every day.*
For giving me the opportunity to live,
*   To have a family, and to give*
All that I have in serving those I love.
*   I am thankful especially to Him above.*

My Father gave me eyes that I might see
*   All the beauty in this life and into eternity.*
He gave me a heart so that I could love
*   And have feelings of compassionate Christlike love.*
He gave me ears that I might hear
*   His whisperings and promptings and all good cheer.*

My Father gave me hands, that I might toil
*   And provide a living, for those I love, from the soil.*
He gave me legs and feet that I might walk
*   Uprightly before Him above,*
And lips and a mouth that I might talk,
*   And teach the kindness of His love.*

The Lord uses music to touch our hearts.
To provide the proper setting to inspire us.
He uses the written and spoken word to touch our souls
And help each of us desire to achieve eternal goals.
Our Father has given us a life and the opportunity
To be with those we love for all eternity.

Christmas comes but once a year
It is a time to remember the birth of our Savior.
The cards and gifts we give, and receive,
Are only important if we really believe.
They are given, and received, in special love
As tokens and remembrances of our Savior's love.

The kind of love the Lord has for us
Is the love that we should have for everyone!

Ethan

Christmas Joy

The birth of a child is even more special
When it happens on Christmas Day.
No other present could be more meaningful
To a parent, grandparent, brother or sister.

The fellowship of friends, the companionship of family,
Sleigh rides, snowball fights, touch football games,
Dinner with all the trimmings, parlor and board games,
Caroling, music and glad tidings in the air.

A time to be thankful; a time to share!
A time to reminisce; a time to care!
A time to rejoice; a time to laugh!
A time to touch; a time to hug and cry!
A time to be with loved ones; a time to build memories!
A time of peace; a time of joy!

Journal entry of Johnny Maverick
December 25, 1973

Chapter Fourteen

Farewell

Tuesday, December 26, 1950

Before breakfast, Samuel remarked to Sara, "I sure am hungry. I don't think I can make it through another one of Papa Allen's Bible readings."

A light went on in Sara's head. "Let's hide Papa Allen's Bible."

No one noticed the children sneak into the drawing room and take the Bible from its normal place near Dr. Allen's chair. They slipped upstairs and hid it underneath the pillow on the doctor's bed.

"Papa Allen will find it tonight after we are all gone," Sara giggled.

Breakfast was ready, and the occupants and guests of the Bradford Inn, except for Molly and her baby, were all seated together. The mood was somewhat somber. The guests all needed to be on their way. Ethan announced that following breakfast, he would make another trip to the telegraph office. He would send telegrams advising when each guest was expected to arrive at his or her destination.

Dr. Allen asked Millicent to retrieve his Bible. A few moments later, she returned from the drawing room and announced, "Papa, I cannot find the Bible. It is not in its place."

Sam and Sara giggled quietly, unnoticed by the others except for Laura, who advised them firmly and quietly. "Hush!"

Dr. Allen proceeded without his Bible. "In the Gospel according to St. John, chapter fifteen, verse twelve, the Lord says, 'This is my commandment, That ye love one another, as I have loved you.'"

Dr. Allen paused for a moment. He extended his hands and said, "Let's all hold hands." He then offered a prayer: "Father, we thank thee for every member of our family. We have a large family of which everyone is a vital part. As the patriarch of this family, I know where each family member is. We thank thee, Father, for sending us thy son, who taught us by his own example how we should live. Help us now, we pray, that we all will continue to follow him. May we all be together forever, even the two little tykes, who hid my Bible under my pillow. May this home always be a refuge for our family and any weary traveler. We thank thee for our guests and for allowing us to be together these few precious hours. We thank thee for the food of which we are about to partake. We pray in the name of our Savior, Jesus Christ, amen."

Talk was minimal during breakfast. All of the guests really felt that they were a part of Dr. Allen's family. They knew that they would always be welcome in his home. They were richly blessed by the new friendships that they had made during the previous thirty-eight hours and by all they had experienced together. Love radiated throughout the inn and throughout the village of Ashton. All the guests knew this was a special place to which they would return often.

Following breakfast, the men packed the automobiles. Logan and Laura planned to reunite that evening at Laura's parents' home in St. Albans. Logan would pay his respects to his friends in Stowe and say his final good-bye to Jan Sommers.

Ethan returned from Waterbury and announced that the roads would be cleared by noon. He also reported that good weather conditions prevailed throughout northern Vermont and were expected to remain that way for the next week.

Johnny was concerned about Molly being able to travel. He wondered if he and Molly should wait another day or two. Molly assured him that she would be all right to make the short trip to her parents' home. Johnny made the rear seat of their automobile into a bed so Molly could lie down with the baby. Dr. Allen checked her over and said she would be fine.

After a light lunch of sandwiches, cookies, pie, milk, and apple cider, everyone said their good-byes.

Dr. Allen's last words to all the guests were, "You are always welcome here. Please return to Ashton often, and always remember to love one another."

Farewell

Was it only by chance they met,
  Strangers brought together by a storm?
Happenstance, or was it meant to be?
  Lives entwined, never to be the same again!

Imagine, Laura without Logan,
  How lost they both would be.
Was it meant to be for Johnny and Molly,
  Their baby being delivered by Dr. Allen?

If Frank and Martha had not been
  Guests at the Bradford Inn,
Would they have ever discovered
  The peace and happiness they both now felt?

What a tragedy for Fordham and Henry,
  If they had missed being with little Mary!
What a misfortune for all the travelers,
  If they had missed Christmas in Ashton!

If the guests had not met Dr. Allen, Millicent,
  Ethan, Constance, Sabrina and Mary
And experienced the love of the carolers,
  Would their lives have remained the same?

Farewells are difficult enough,
  But this one will be sweet.
Friendships made! Memories to cherish forever!
  How fortunate they all have been!

The travelers will now go their separate ways.
  Their hearts are full! Tears fill their eyes.
This farewell is not the end, but only the beginning,
  Of many returns to Ashton!

Journal entry of Serelda Maverick
November 18, 1951

Chapter Fifteen

Ashton Revisited

Monday, January 1, 1951

Logan had joined Laura and her children at her parents' home in St. Albans, where they spent the remaining days of December. They happy couple began preparations for a June wedding. After breakfast on New Year's Day, Logan, Laura, Samuel, and Sara left St. Albans to return to Boston. They planned to stop in Ashton and spend a few hours with Dr. Allen and his family. Samuel rode with Logan in his Cadillac, while Laura and Sara followed in Laura's Plymouth.

The weather was pleasant when they turned up the road to Ashton. It was a clear day. The sun was shining, and the snow sparkled with the sun's reflection. Logan and Laura had almost missed the road because the sign pointing to the village was hard to read. It was weather-beaten and needed painting. Logan, Laura, Samuel, and Sara were not prepared for what they were about to see. When they came to Ashton, there was something terribly wrong.

How could the village have changed so much in just six days?

The beautiful white-and-green trimmed Bradford Inn was unpainted. In fact, the paint appeared to have long since peeled off because of years of neglect. The windows were boarded up, and a sign posted on the front door read: "No Trespassing! Violators will be prosecuted!" The barn in the back was in shambles, and silence prevailed, except for the sounds of loose boards flapping in the wind. There were no familiar sounds of the barnyard animals.

They looked toward the village of Ashton. It looked like a ghost town! The streets were void of people. Buildings that stood six days ago were gone. Only a few homes and stores remained, and they too were unpainted and appeared to be abandoned. Few trees and bushes remained where many had stood only a few days before. Ghostly quietness prevailed! This was a far contrast from the sounds of Christmas that filled the homes and streets of Ashton just days ago. Logan and Laura were in shock!

"Where is Dr. Allen and everyone else?" cried Laura with tears streaming down her cheeks.

Logan could not speak. He just shook his head. After a long silence, he commented, "Right place, wrong century! As a judge, I know I am a sane man! There has to be an explanation! I know I was in that home six days ago and that we spent Christmas there! I know there were people living there! We touched them! We hugged them! We interacted with them! They were alive! They were real! They loved us, and we loved them! I know all this happened, and so do you, Laura, and so does Samuel and Sara! Wait here while I check inside."

The front door was padlocked. It was apparent from the footprints in the snow that others had recently been there. Logan followed the tracks around the side of the inn to a place where some boards had been removed. This appeared to have been done to gain entrance, through a boarded-up window, into what he knew to be the dining room. The room was empty now, except for dust, spiderwebs, and a few mice scurrying around. Logan could see that the rest of the inn was some-what dark, but enough light crept in through the cracks in the boarded-up windows. After exploring the remainder of the inn, he returned to Laura, Samuel, and Sara.

"No one inside! The rooms are all empty! The furniture is all gone! I found a newspaper on the floor dated 1909. Other than that, there is just dust, dirt, spiderwebs, and mice. Yet, as remarkable as it may seem, here is the music box that Dr. Allen gave Sara—the one she accidentally left behind. When I went into the drawing room, there was a beam of light directly on it. Otherwise, I would have missed it. It is just as shiny as it was six days ago. There is not a speck of dust on it. Funny thing, though—the name of the maker and the year are in-scribed on the bottom of the box: Fondorff Music Company, Boston, 1854. I examined the music box when Dr. Allen gave it to Sara last week. I don't remember that inscription being on it. This does not make sense! As a matter of fact, nothing makes sense! I have a strong feeling that the music box was left there for Sara."

A bewildered Laura just shook her head. Samuel and Sara did not understand everything either, but Sara was thrilled to have her music box back. Neither Logan nor Laura could ex-plain what happened to Dr. Allen and his family.

"I know the answer," Sara hinted. "They all went to heaven."

Logan suggested they explore the village. As he, Laura, Samuel, and Sara walked through the streets, they saw what they had already surmised. There was little left of the village and no sign of habitation. What could have possibly happened to the quaint little village of Ashton with which they had all fallen in love—the place they vowed to return to often?

When they came to the church, they saw some smoke com-ing from the parsonage next door. There they met Billy Ebbs, who explained that he was the only resident left in Ashton.

Billy said he was born in Ashton in 1887. He related that there were only a few families living in the village when his parents settled there in the late 1870s. By 1910, everyone had either died or left, except for his mother, sister, and himself. His sister eventually moved away and never returned. His mother died in 1933. Billy had lived there alone ever since.

Billy stated, "The others said you'd come."

"Others?" asked Logan.

"Yep, the others," Billy said frankly. "The Parsons from someplace down Boston way—brothers who said their ma is buried up in the cemetery on the hill. Then Mr. and Mrs. Masters—yep, that was their name—they come. Mrs. Masters is the niece of the Parsons. Her ma was their half sister—yep, their half sister. Then come a real likable young couple who had a baby."

"Johnny and Molly?" Laura questioned.

Billy Ebbs smiled and went on, "Yep, the ballplayer and his missus. Yep, they all said you folks would come. Funny thing is no folk ever come here anymore and then all you folks show up in just the last couple of days. All the others have folks buried in that there cemetery. They all sure did a lot of cryin'. I 'spect you'll want to mosey on up there. I reckon you'll find your folks up there."

Logan and Laura had been trying to comprehend all of Mr. Ebbs's mumbling. Was he inferring that some—or all—of them were related to one another? Logan was not aware that he had any family buried here. *It must be Laura's family,* he thought. Her father did remark that some members of his mother's family were from this area, but he did not know much about them, since his mother died several days after he was born. None of her family ever came around. He remembered hearing that she did have some family out in Texas.

"Laura, could you somehow be related to Johnny?" asked Logan.

Laura, who was still in shock, just shook her head. "I don't know."

Logan asked Billy Ebbs if he had spent Christmas in Ashton.

"Nope!" was Billy's answer. He explained that he never spends Christmas in Ashton. His only sister lives in Burlington. He always went there to spend the holiday with her. He stated that he left about noon on Christmas Eve and returned about the same time on December 27, because he never likes to overstay his welcome.

"Yep, I guess you'll want to mosey on up to that there cemetery now," he added. "I'll show you folks the way."

Logan, Laura, Samuel, and Sara followed Billy to the cemetery, which was located several hundred yards behind the church on a small hill overlooking the village. A blanket of snow covered the cemetery, but most of the tombstones were visible. Footprints in the snow were clear evidence that others had recently been there. It was easy to see where they had walked.

Logan and Laura's attention quickly centered on a large, tall stone with the surname Allen written in large, bold letters. They stood in amazement as they read: "Dr. Bradford Allen, born 1769, died 1862, beloved father and physician, founder of the village of Ashton, 1796." There were two other names on the same stone: "Temperance Maverick, wife of Dr. B. Allen, born 1775, died 1823" and "Jane Buck, wife of Dr. B. Allen, born 1800, died 1849"

There was also a large stone a few feet away with the surname Adams on it. Two names were inscribed on it, "Dr. Samuel Adams, born 1843, died 1912" and "Patience Allen, wife of Dr. S. Adams, born 1841, died 1931."

Laura just shook her head and muttered, "Dr. Allen and Patience are dead?"

"Yes!" Logan answered. "The evidence certainly points that

direction." Logan's analytical mind was sorting through the events of the previous week and comparing them to what he had witnessed during the past hour.

The Ashton he fell in love with just a week ago was out of the 1800s. There had been nothing in the inn to suggest otherwise. He recalled his conversation with Johnny, who agreed that everything about the village was quaint. All the guests were enamored with the inn, the village, the villagers, and the countryside. They reflected how fortunate Dr. Allen and his fellow villagers were to be able to enjoy such a quiet life in such a tranquil atmosphere. They had all looked beyond the clothing that Dr. Allen, his family, and the villagers wore. Everything they saw or heard suggested that the inn and the village and its occupants were from another period in time, but reason did not prevail at Christmastime. Not only Dr. Allen and his family extended love and fellowship but also all of the villagers of Ashton. The reason why was now rapidly becoming apparent.

Billy Ebbs continued, "Yep, I buried Patience Adams back in '31. She's dead all right. Her pa died long 'fore I was ever born. He found the village of Ashton. He had a big farm. He gave the village a big chunk of it. He asked a lot of folks to move here. Ashton was busy at one time. He was a doc. People say he borned most of the folk buried here, 'cept my ma and pa and a few others. He lived in the inn."

"We know," added Logan.

Logan noticed five smaller stones. "Look here, Laura. Dr. Allen and his second wife, Jane, had five additional children: George, born 1826, died 1832; Thomas, born 1829, died 1832; Rachel, born and died 1832; Bradford Jr., born 1836, died 1849; Alexander, born 1840, died 1849. Very sad—they all died as children: three in 1832, and two in 1849, the same year as his wife, Jane. I wonder if they died from epidemics."

"Yep, cholera!" interjected Billy Ebbs.

Nearby was a very large stone with the surname Buck. Six names were on this stone: "Col. Aaron Buck, born 1785, died 1832; Millicent Allen, wife of Col. A. Buck, born 1793, died 1864; children of A. and M. Buck: Rachel, dau., born 1810, died 1811; Aaron, son, born 1813, died 1832; Sarah, dau., born 1819, died 1832; Adam, son, born 1823, died 1832."

"Millicent and her family," commented Logan. "She must have suffered so much. After burying an infant daughter, she buried three children and her husband in 1832. My admiration for her continues to grow."

"I just can't believe she's dead too," added Laura. "Colonel Aaron Buck was the silversmith who made the silver-plated brush and comb sets that were in my and Sara's stockings. We will cherish them even more now. I just can't believe everyone from Dr. Allen's family is dead!"

"That's what all the others said too!" exclaimed Billy Ebbs. He seemed to be enjoying everyone's shock. "Most 'citement I've had 'round here in a long spell. Folks wonderin' why all these folks is dead. Easy to figure—folks all born over a hun'red years ago, some born back 'fore the Revolutionary War. Cholera hit here in 1832 and again in 1849. Erysipelas hit in 1843, smallpox and varioloid in 1856 and 1857, and scarlet fever in 1874 and 1875. Not much left of Ashton after all that. Nope, not hard to figure."

Then Logan and Laura noticed another large tombstone with the surname Case on it. There were two names on it: "Maj. Ethan Case, born 1832, died 1864; Constance Alden, wife of Maj. E. Case, born 1836, died 1888."

"Not Ethan and Constance too!" exclaimed Laura with tears streaming down her face.

"Bull's-eye!" exclaimed Billy Ebbs. "Killed at Gettysburg during the Civil War! My pa said Mr. Case's body is not buried here—said he was buried at Gettysburg. His missus died a year after I was born. My pa buried her. Pa said Mr. Case's youngins had Mr. Case's name put on the tombstone when they had it made up for his missus. My pa was the caretaker of the cemetery—my job now, even though there's no one left to pay me. We used to get some money from Mr. Case's youngin Jonathan Case, who lived down in Texas. He must have died back in the early thirties 'cuz that's when his money quit comin'. That ballplayer with the missus and baby—Johnny Maverick—yep, figured out that the Cases were his great-grandma and great-grandpa."

"My great-grandparents too!" exclaimed Laura. "My father's mother was a Case. Johnny and I are cousins somehow. That would make Millicent our great-great-great- grandmother. That means we are both descendants of Dr. Allen."

"Yep, that young couple, the Mavericks, they figured out they were some sort of kin too," added Billy Ebbs in amusement. "Seems like Mrs. Maverick's ma was raised up by old Doc Adams and his missus."

"Patience?" Laura questioned.

"Yep, old Doc Allen's youngin, Patience," answered Billy. "Seems Patience was some kind of an aunt or somethin'. Patience helped raise Mrs. Maverick after Mrs. Maverick's ma, Rachel, died when Mrs. Maverick was a baby. Mrs. Maverick said she was only nine years old when her Aunt Patty died, back in '31. She 'membered comin' to the cemetery for the burial. Yep, that's when Mrs. Maverick really got all choked up. She just sat down on that there grave of Patience Adams and cried like a baby—right there in the snow. Yep, she said all that she had left of her Aunt Patty was a music box left to her in her aunt's will. She just kept saying the same thing over and over again: 'I didn't know! I didn't know! I didn't know! I didn't know!' She was a real basket case, yep."

Logan noticed two smaller tombstones next to the graves of Ethan and Constance: "Millicent, dau. of E. and C. Case, born and died 1859; Priscilla, dau. of E. and C. Case, born 1864, died 1934."

Logan commented, "These are the daughters of Ethan and Constance."

Then he noticed a large tombstone also with the surname Case on it. There were four names on it: "Henry Case, born 1807, died 1849; Temperance Buck, wife of H. Case, born 1815, died 1849; Aaron, son of H. and T. Case, born 1834, died 1843; Prudence, dau. of H. and T. Case, born 1837, died 1843."

Billy Ebbs blurted out, "Henry and Temperance Case was the pa and ma of Ethan Case. They died of cholera in 1849. Erysipelas hit here in 1843. It took their two youngins here."

Logan commented, "My heart goes out to Dr. Allen and Millicent. After losing so many of their family in 1832, one can only imagine the heartache they felt in 1843 and 1849. I cannot begin to comprehend their grief. Ethan was only seventeen years old, Sabrina was nine, and Mary was six when they lost their parents. No wonder they matured so quickly. Patience was only eight. Not only did she lose her mother and her older brothers, Bradford Jr. and Alexander, she also lost those people whom she loved very dearly. Constance lost her parents when she was seven years old. That would have been about 1843. These people all became her family. In 1849, she would have been about thirteen years old—a very difficult age to have to endure this tragic loss of family again in her young life."

So much was racing through Logan's mind. He knew this would be a long day and sleep would come slowly that night. He knew that Laura was having a difficult time comprehending all they had discovered since returning to Ashton. She was suffering from shock. He was concerned about her, but he knew she would be okay.

Logan was also concerned for the children, Samuel and Sara. They seemed to understand that Dr. Allen and his family were dead and buried in the cemetery. The children loved Dr. Allen and had been looking forward to seeing him again. Logan knew they would have many questions, and he and Laura would need to spend a lot of time helping them understand all they had experienced in the last eight days. Would the children feel the grief of the deaths of Dr. Allen and his family? Or would they be able to understand how fortunate they all had been to be able to spend a few precious hours together, getting to really know one another?

Logan noticed more footprints in the snow. They led to a very tall and stately stone that had an angel made of iron mounted on the top. The angel was dull green in appearance but magnificent to behold. The inscription read: "Mary Case, beloved wife of F. W. Parsons IV, born Mar. 3, 1843, died Dec. 25, 1883." The grave was encased in a wrought iron fence, and there was a stone bench at the base of the grave.

"Little Mary was the mother of Fordham and Henry," stated Logan. "That's why she attached herself so much to them."

Billy Ebbs added, "'Twas the Parsons brothers' pa who made 'rangements with the village to have my pa be the caretaker of the cemetery. Yep, their pa gave a lot of money for all this. He wished fresh flowers put on his missus' grave every day when flowers were in bloom 'round here. Money ran out a long time ago, but I keep on bringin' flowers. Yep, I 'member my pa tellin' me that old man Parsons was some kind of a big college man down Boston way.

"He only come two times. First time was when he brung his missus to be buried, and then many years later, he come back. I was 'bout ten years old at the time, and I 'member that day real clear. Yep, was in the middle of winter, and old man Parsons sat on that there bench, alone, all day. Yep, must have been least eight or ten hours that he just sat there. Anyway, 'bout dusk, he come down to our house. He had a small chest with him. He asked my pa to bury the chest next to his missus's grave. Yep, I guess my pa forgot to bury it 'cuz I found it years later in our attic. 'Twas padlocked.

"I forgot 'bout the chest 'til day 'fore yesterday, when 'em Parsons brothers was here. They just sat up here all day, too, on this here bench. I left 'em alone. Yep, while they was up here, I got to 'memberin' about the chest in the attic. Figured they just might want to have it 'cuz it's rightfully theirs. Yep, they was so 'cited. They couldn't wait 'til they got home to open it. I got some tools and broke the lock off for 'em. Nothin' much in the chest—just an old wedding dress, some old diaries, letters, pictures, newspaper clippings, and a music box."

"Like this one?" interjected an excited Sara as she held up her music box for Billy Ebbs to see. She opened it, and music filled the air.

"Yep, same music, and same kind of box. Yours is real shiny, though. Looks just like it, 'cept that music box in the chest was all tarnished," commented Billy Ebbs. "Well, anyway, the Parsons was real 'cited. It was about that time that Mr. and Mrs. Masters showed up. It seems Mrs. Masters..."

"Martha," interjected Laura.

"Yep, Martha," replied Billy Ebbs. "Seems she had a music box too—like the one in the chest. Says it 'longed to her ma, Anne. Yep, Anne was her name. Mrs. Masters—I mean, Martha—said that Anne was raised up thinkin' she was the oldest youngin of her ma and pa. Later she found out that she was the illegitimate youngin of the sister of the woman she thought was her ma. Sabrina Fowler was the name of the woman who raised her up. The music box Martha had was given to Sabrina one Christmas by her great-grandpa, Doc Allen. Anyway, Sabrina gave her music box to Anne, who gave it to Martha on the day that she and Frank Masters got hitched. The music box was stolen while they was on their honeymoon. Anyway, the music box mysteriously showed up the day 'fore yesterday in the old Bradford Inn."

"I can believe that," interjected Logan.

"Well, anyways," continued Billy Ebbs, "there was a letter

in the Parsonses' chest addressed to 'Anne Marie Fowler, Concord, New Hampshire.' The letter was from Mary Parsons. It was never mailed. The letter said that it would never be mailed in her lifetime, or even after her death. Mary Parsons writ in the letter that she was the real ma of Anne Marie Fowler. She gave Anne to her sister Sabrina 'cuz she loved Anne and didn't want her made fun of and branded as an illegitimate youngin. Mary was alone when Anne was born and didn't have no way to fend for Anne either. Well, anyway, Anne Fowler was really the half sister of Fordham and Henry Parsons. All I know is that after they figured all this out, the Masterses and the Parsonses was doing a lot of huggin' and cryin.'"

Logan interrupted, "I remember seeing a family Bible once that listed my grandmother's name as Mary Fowler, and her mother's name was Sabrina. Both my grandmother and great-grandmother died before I was born, but I have been to their graves in New Hampshire. Now, I know why Sabrina, Constance, and Ethan were so interested in us, Laura."

"And Mary, Millicent, Patience, and Dr. Allen," added Laura.

"Mama, look!" exclaimed an excited Sara. "What does it say?" She showed her mother and Logan an additional inscription on the bottom of the music box. It had not been there previously. The inscription read: "Given to Constance Alden on Christmas Day 1854 by Dr. Bradford Allen. Given to Sara Winchester on Christmas Day 1950 by her fifth-great-grandfather, Dr. Bradford Allen, with the permission of her great-great-grandmother, Constance Alden Case."

Laura explained to her daughter, "Sara, it says that both Papa Allen and Constance love you very much."

Logan commented, "Now I know what Dr. Allen's gift to all of us was. We didn't go back in time. The past came to us. Dr. Allen and his family brought us all together. They each had a special interest in us, and there were reasons for bringing us together. They helped us. Without them, we wouldn't have discovered one another, and we wouldn't have discovered Ashton. Now we know why they loved us so much. They turned their hearts to us. Now we must turn our hearts to them and not forget them and all they have done and sacrificed for each of us."

The Cemetery on the Hill

This hard and cold stone bench
  Is where I have sat for many hours now,
Thinking, reflecting, and pondering what is in my heart,
  As I look upon the tombstones,
That mark the graves of my ancestors, and their families.
  Their mortal remains lie deep below.

Silence now fills the air, except for the
  Chirping of birds, and the whistling of the wind.
The tombstones are old and difficult to read;
  Worn and ravaged by time and nature's elements.
An ocean of tears once covered this sacred place,
  The resting place of my forefathers.

I am thankful that they lived and am grateful
  For the gift of heritage, they have given me.
Respect, peace, love, thankfulness - fill my heart!
  Without them, I would not be!
Free now, from the bonds of their temporal existence,
  Their immortal souls have long since departed.

Their blood flows through my veins.
  Their traits, I have inherited.
Although, they have provided me with a firm foundation,
  I am not, just, a composite of my progenitors.
It is up to me, to build my own life.
  To create my own destiny!

My life will stand as a testament to them,
  Those from whom, I have descended.
I may not have the privilege to come here often.
  However, I will always remember this hallowed ground
And those who lie buried here. I owe them so very much!
  I celebrate their lives! My heart is full!

This cemetery on the hill
  Is only a temporal memorial.
A thousand years from now, it will be no more.
  That is not a tragedy, but the way of this earth.
There is a superior resting place for our loved ones.
  It lies on a higher hill!

Journal entry of Fordham Parsons
December 30, 1950

What Makes A House A Home

The house is empty now,
  Ghostly quietness prevails.
Unpainted and abandoned, cold!
  Weather beaten and neglected!
Boarded up windows, furniture gone!
  Cobwebs, dust, a rat or two!

Close your eyes, and remember back.
  Years, perhaps, a war or two.
The smell of freshly baked pie or bread!
  Laughter, chatter, and crying!
Children playing, a cat, a dog, a bird,
  Mom and Dad, Grandpa and Grandma!

What makes a house a home?
  A family!

Journal entry of Logan Emory
June 2, 1988

In the Midst of Angels

With sounds of Christmas in the air,
  Wreaths with holly and decorations everywhere.
The angelic family and their guests, together mingling;
  We were blessed when a heavenly choir came singing.

The night air was still, full of peace, calm and love.
  The stars shone brightly in the heavens above.
The full moon reigned, majestically, that night.
  Angels were present, with us, to witness the sight.

We listened to the story, of that wondrous night long ago,
  When God sent His Son to live with us, here below.
We heard Christmas hymns sung of an era past.
  Love filled our hearts; we prayed the feeling would last.

We were blessed again, on Christmas Day,
  With the gifts of love that came our way.
And to this day, it's still hard to believe,
  Of all the love that was ours to give and receive.

Too short the time, our visit too brief.
  All that took place was well beyond belief.
Little did we realize, during our special Christmas in Ashton,
  That we were in the midst of angels.

Many years have past, fond memories remain,
  Of the villagers, the carolers, Constance and Ethan,
Of Dr. Allen, Millicent, Patience, Sabrina and Mary.
  We, now, know – we were in the midst of angels!

Journal entry of Logan Emory
April 4, 1980

Dr. Bradford Allen

A taller man I know not.
Not measured by height,
But by moral character,
Conviction and acts of kindness.

A leader of men was he,
Who yet allowed small children,
To take him by their tiny hands
Into their worlds of fantasy.

Physician by profession,
Farmer and innkeeper by choice,
Patriarch of a family,
Founder of a village.

One who would not let
The elements of nature:
Snow, fierce winds, bitter cold, ice and rain,
Deter him from his work.

Counselor to the forlorn,
Servant to his fellow men,
Healer to many, friend to everyone.
Sure were his hands, gentle were his words.

Firm was his handshake,
Benevolent was his nature,
A man of great strength, courage,
Faith, hope and charity.

Many years from now,
It will always be said of him.
Everyone always looked up to Dr. Allen,
A taller man we know not.

Journal entry of Millicent Allen Buck
March 8, 1863

My Life

I live and freely give my life,
    For my God,
    For my family,
      Past, present and future.
    For my friends,
    For my neighbor,
    For my community,
    For my country,
    For the stranger,
      That I may not pass him by.
And to humanity,
    That I, too, might leave my life
    Engraved upon the pages of time.

Journal entry of Dr. Bradford Allen
September 7, 1849

Chapter Sixteen

Strangers No More

Several weeks later, Logan took Laura to Arlington, Virginia, to meet his father, Hon. Harrison Logan Emory Jr., United States Supreme Court justice. Justice Emory disclosed a startling family secret.

"Laura, you mentioned that your late husband, Samuel Winchester, was from Portland, Maine. When I asked you about his siblings, you said there were none—that he was adopted and that his parents were in their mid-fifties when they adopted him. Were the names of Samuel's parents, by any chance, William and Lillian Winchester?"

Laura replied, "Yes, they were. How did you know?"

Logan gripped Laura's hand tightly.

Justice Emory continued, "Logan, I am about to break a promise that I made to your mother on the day she agreed to be my wife. I remade the promise to her on the day she passed away. I must now break that promise because you and Laura need to know this. My wife was a child when her father died, and she was only sixteen when her mother passed away. All of her family members were dead except for her first cousin, Rachel Adams Seymour, and a very elderly aunt who had raised Rachel, Patience Adams."

Laura interrupted, "Molly's mother and Patience!"

Justice Emory looked perplexed and then asked, "You're familiar with these people?"

Logan answered for Laura, "Dad, it's a long story, and we will try to explain later. Yes, Laura and I both are familiar with Rachel and Patience. We know Rachel's daughter, Molly Maverick. We have been to the cemetery where Patience Adams and her family are buried. These people came into our lives a few weeks ago. Please, go on with what you were about to tell us about Mother."

Justice Emory continued, "As I was saying, your mother was orphaned when she was just sixteen. A close family friend adopted her younger brother. Both Rachel and Patience wanted your mother to come live with them, but she wanted her independence and ran away to Boston. She worked as a waitress in a small café near my law office. She became involved with a married man and found herself... pregnant."

Logan gasped.

Justice Emory continued, "Your mother knew I was an attorney and asked me for help. She wanted to make sure her baby would go to a good family. I made arrangements for the infant to be adopted by my aunt Lillian and her husband, William Morris Winchester. They were both in their forties when they married and had no children. They were considered too old to adopt a child by all of the adoption agencies. I pulled a few strings, and the Winchesters legally adopted the baby boy born to your mother in 1917. At that time, Lillian and William were both in their mid-fifties. They named their son Samuel William Winchester."

Laura gasped.

Justice Emory continued, "Yes, Laura, their son was your

Samuel, the half brother that you, Logan, never knew you had. I frequented the café more often and began to court your mother. We were married nearly a year after Samuel was born. My aunt and uncle were understandably upset by our marriage. They refused to have further contact with us. My wife requested that I never tell any of our children about Samuel.

"For your mother's sake, Logan, I was happy that Lillian and William did not bring their son to our home or to any other family gatherings. It would have been most difficult on your mother. Samuel's name was never mentioned in our home. Even though my aunt cut herself off from the rest of our family, no one ever suspected that your mother was Samuel's natural mother.

"I do believe that if your mother were living today and sitting here beside me, she would be the one telling you this. For I believe that under the circumstances, she would want you to know. Laura, I never met Samuel, and it wasn't until recently that I found out that he had died and left a family. Out of respect to my wife's wishes, I never tried to contact you."

Silence filled the room. Laura was the first to speak. "I would like to think that Samuel and his natural mother are happy that Logan and I will be married."

Sara and Sam then entered the room. Logan, Laura, Sam, and Sara told Justice Emory about Christmas in Ashton with Dr. Allen and his family. They told him about their return to Ashton and the trip to the cemetery. They wondered if Justice Emory would question their sanity. Upon the conclusion of their relating their cherished experience, Justice Emory excused himself and left them alone for several minutes.

When Justice Emory returned, he had a veneer-finish wooden box in his hands. He carefully set it down on the coffee table in front of Logan, Laura, Samuel, and Sara. When Justice Emory opened the top of the box, it revealed a very old Bible that was housed safely in the velvet-lined box. Justice Emory very carefully removed the aged Bible from the box and held it, with great respect, in his hands.

Samuel and Sara exclaimed in unison, "Papa Allen's Bible!"

Samuel continued, "The one we hid under his pillow!"

"Yes, children," added Justice Emory, "Dr. Bradford Allen's family Bible. In addition to containing the word of God, this Bible has several pages in it that list all of Dr. Allen's family and several generations of his descendants. It contains a record of their births, marriages, and deaths. When Dr. Allen died in 1862, the family Bible went to his daughter Millicent. When she died two years later, it was passed on to Millicent's younger sister and Dr. Allen's only living child, Patience Adams. She had no children of her own. The child she raised, Rachel Adams Seymour, died in 1923. Patience, fearing her own days were numbered, passed the cherished family Bible on to her beloved niece, Cynthia Anne Kidder Emory, my wife.

"Now I am passing it on to you, Logan and Laura. I believe that this would be the wish of Dr. Allen.

"Logan, you knew Patience Adams as a child. The last time she was in our home was shortly before your mother passed away, in 1927, when you were just eight years old. You would remember her as Aunt Pit Pat, which was your mother's nickname for her, and that's what we also fondly called her. I knew her well and remember her talking many times about her sister, Millicent, and her father, Dr. Allen, and about life in Ashton with Ethan, Constance, Sabrina, and Mary. You have described these people exactly as I remember Aunt Pit Pat describing them. If you all had not known them yourselves, you would never have been able to describe them as clearly as you have."

Strangers No More

The homeless stranger, we turn away:
  "I will help him some other day."
The elderly neighbor, we choose not to know:
  "She will expect me to shovel her snow."
The crippled child, the forgotten schoolmate:
  "If I am friend to him, I will always be late."

Have we ever thought who they may be,
  If we could open our hearts and our eyes to see.
Could they be a distant cousin or the grandparent we never met?
  Or the child of a long forgotten friend? Or, sadder yet,
Could they be the half brother, or sister, we never knew we had?
  Or perhaps, they could be our own mom or dad!

We never know, when we begin each day,
  The opportunities that will come our way.
Perhaps, a prayer, a scripture or two
  Will help open our hearts and our eyes anew.
We never know, who we may meet today,
  Perhaps, the child we gave away!

The stranger may be........no stranger at all!

Journal entry of Logan Emory
February 6, 1972

Logan

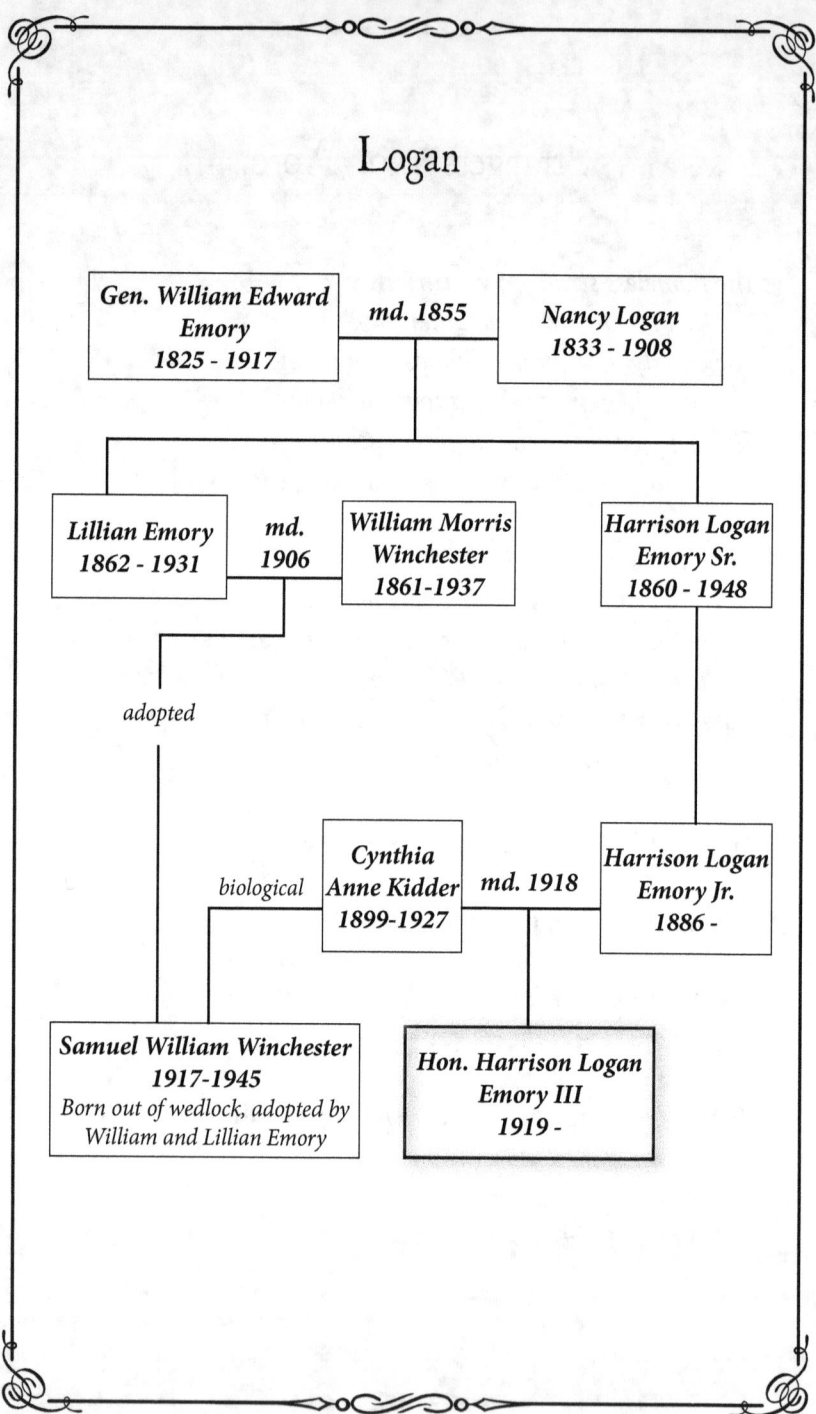

Chapter Seventeen

Epilogue

Tuesday, December 24, 1996

"That was a great story, Grandpa," commented sixteen-year-old Laura Winchester.

"I liked Millicent the best," exclaimed eighteen-year-old Millicent Winchester.

Patience Ormsby, age sixteen, always the diplomat, added, "Millicent was a special lady, but so was Patience, and I like hearing about her."

"I think it was terrible that Grandma used to be poor and had to work so hard. I am happy she and Grandpa fell in love and got married. It was like Cinderella and Prince Charming, and they lived happily ever after," remarked twelve-year-old Charlene Emory.

"Dad, I like hearing this story every time you tell it," commented forty-four-year-old Sabrina Emory Givens.

"Father, I wish I could have met Papa Allen, Ethan, and everyone else," added Cynthia Emory Rose, the second of Logan and Laura's triplets, born in 1952.

"They were all wonderful people. I wish you, and everyone else in our family, could have known them and loved them as your father, Samuel, Sara, and I were able to," commented seventy-four-year-old Laura Winchester Emory.

"I didn't like Mr. Fitzgerald. He was mean to Grandma," piped in seven-year-old Harrison Logan Emory V.

"Can you imagine how upset Mr. Fitzgerald was when Dad called him and informed him that Mom was not returning to work?" laughed thirty-nine-year-old Bradford Allen Emory.

"He was really upset, but he still came to our wedding," chuckled seventy-seven-year-old Logan Emory.

"I am proud that I am a descendant of Dr. Bradford Allen," commented thirty-year-old Donna Emory Anderson, the youngest of Logan and Laura's ten children. "I am thankful that I was born in Ashton and that I was raised in this special home, in this wonderful family, and in this beautiful village. Greg and I are thrilled that we have been able to return to Ashton, buy the newspaper, and build a home here. This is where we want to raise our family."

Logan looked at his watch. He exclaimed, "Oh my! I see that it is nearly time for us to go. We don't want to be late."

Logan and Laura and their children, grandchildren, and one great-grandson—fifty people in all—had been seated in the drawing room of the family home, the Bradford Inn in Ashton, Vermont. The inn looked as it had exactly forty-six years before. As the family began filing out of the inn, the streets of Ashton were quickly filling up as others throughout the village were headed in the same direction: to the center of the village. Ashton was even more beautiful than it was when Logan and Laura were first introduced to it. There were more homes and many more residents. Over eight hundred people made their way into the spacious Ashton Civic Auditorium.

Logan made his way to the podium at the head table, where ninety-eight-year-old Frank Masters and his eighty-seven-year-old wife, Martha, were already seated. Laura took her place next to Logan. Also seated at the head table were Johnny and Molly Maverick. Louisa Parsons Cavendish and her husband, Michael, sat at the head table, representing the Parsons family.

Logan addressed the large gathering. "On this very day forty-six years ago, some of us were given the opportunity to spend a remarkable Christmas as the guests of Dr. Bradford Allen and his family. Little did we realize then how much they all really did love us. They brought us together for a purpose. Their incredible kindness touched us and changed our lives forever. They taught us to love one another, and they taught us that we are all a vital part of their family. Dr. Allen loved his family, and he loved Ashton. Our village thrives today as a testament to him. Over five hundred of us here today are direct descendants, or spouses of descendants, of Dr. Bradford Allen. The rest of you have been added into his family because you have chosen to make Ashton your home.

"Dr. Allen taught us that a family that eats together, plays together, and prays together will always be together! Let us all join hands."

Ashton

Quiet meadows, tranquillity,
　　Birds chirping, flowers in bloom,
Blue sky, the snow covered ground,
　　The green mountains of Vermont.

Indians, settlers, 1776, freedom, farms,
　　A dream, a village, a covered bridge,
Courtships, marriages, families, children playing,
　　Picnics, parades, ballgames, people laughing.

Teachers, storekeepers, villagers, travelers,
　　Churches, stores, parks and gardens,
The blacksmith, the silversmith, the potter, the doctor,
　　The Bradford Inn, the school, the newspaper and village hall.

Disease, pestilence, Civil War, death,
　　The cemetery on the hill, the village forgotten,
Empty streets, vacant houses, stores in shambles,
　　Weeds, stillness, the ghosts of times past.

The doctor, his family, a second chance,
　　To reunite his family, to revitalize his dream.
The judge, the widow, her children, the brothers and their niece,
　　The baseball star, his family, brought together for a purpose.

The carolers, their forefathers, the Master of us all,
Gifts of love, answered prayers, the birth of a child.
The hearts of the fathers turned to their children, sharing hearts,
The magic of Christmas, the miracle of love.

A glimpse of the past, a vision for the future,
With love in their hearts and love for their forefathers.
A family committed, and united, to rebuilding the village,
A family reunited, the dream fulfilled!

Kendall H. Williams

Afterword

Author's Notes

The couple that Fordham thought he recognized among the carolers were his grandparents, Temperance Buck and Henry Case. They were the parents of Ethan, Sabrina, and Mary. Temperance was the daughter of Millicent. Many times as a small child, Fordham had been shown a picture of his grandparents by his mother. That picture was in the chest that he and Henry were given at the cemetery.

The person that Fordham thought he saw among the carolers was his father.

The caroler who gave Molly the small wooden box that contained the antique locket was her grandmother, Catherine Anne Fowler. Catherine died in childbirth when she was only sixteen years old. The two small, oval pictures in the locket were of Catherine, taken when she was fifteen, and of her baby, Rachel, Molly's mother. The locket had belonged to Catherine's mother, Sabrina Case Fowler.

The other caroler who Molly noticed looking directly at her, the woman whose face was covered except for her forehead and eyes, was Molly's mother, Rachel, who died when Molly was an infant.

The two carolers to whom Martha and Frank were especially drawn were indeed their children, Franklin Marion Masters Jr. and Frances Anne Masters. The woman who led the twins away was Martha's mother, Anne Marie Fowler Pratt.

The young lady in the Parsons family portrait who Fordham and Henry felt was the sister they never knew was indeed their sister: Anne Marie Fowler Pratt. Martha and Frank recognized her in the portrait as Martha's mother. They had both noticed how strongly Martha's mother resembled Mary Parsons. They decided to wait until a later date to inform Fordham and Henry of their suspected relationship. Their chance meeting at the cemetery gave them the right setting to do this.

Fordham would later reflect, "When I was a child, my mother told me about the Christ Child and taught me to love him. When I was an old man, she helped to restore those feelings in me."

Christmas Day 1854 fell on a Monday. Sabrina was fourteen, Patience was thirteen, and Mary was eleven. They each originally received their music boxes that day. Constance also received a music box that day. Her music box is the same one Sara received on Christmas Day 1950, which also fell on a Monday. Constance is Sara's great-great-grandmother.

Laura and Johnny are both great-grandchildren of Ethan. Laura and Johnny are second cousins. Molly and Logan are both great-grandchildren of Sabrina. Molly and Logan are second cousins. Henry and Fordham are the children of Mary; Martha is the granddaughter of Mary. Ethan, Sabrina, and Mary are the children of Temperance Buck, who is the daughter of Millicent Buck, the daughter of Dr. Bradford Allen.

Laura and Molly are third cousins. Laura and Logan are third cousins. Laura's relationship to Martha is second cousin, once removed. Laura's relationship to Henry and Fordham is first cousin, twice removed.

Logan and Johnny are third cousins. Logan's relationship to Martha is second cousin, once removed. His relationship to Henry and Fordham is first cousin, twice removed.

Molly and Johnny are third cousins. Molly's relationship to Martha is second cousin, once removed. Molly's relationship to Henry and Fordham is first cousin, twice removed.

Johnny's relationship to Martha is second cousin, once removed. His relationship to Henry and Fordham is first cousin, twice removed.

Martha is the niece of Henry and Fordham.

Dr. Bradford Allen is the great-great-grandfather of Henry and Fordham. He is the third-great-grandfather of Martha. He is the fourth-great-grandfather of Laura, Logan, Molly, and Johnny. He is the fifth-great-grandfather of Samuel, Sara, and the baby Bradford Allen Maverick.

Millicent is the great-grandmother of Henry and Fordham. She is the great-great-grandmother of Martha. She is the third-great-grandmother of Laura, Logan, Molly, and Johnny. She is the fourth-great-grandmother of Samuel, Sara, and the baby Bradford Allen Maverick.

Constance is the great-grandmother of Laura and Johnny. She is the great-great-grandmother of Samuel, Sara, and the baby Bradford Allen Maverick.

Frank was fortunate to have married into this special family when he became Martha's husband.

Additional Notes

Behind the Scenes

On Thanksgiving Day, November 28, 1996, I arrived in Cambridge, Massachusetts, in a part of town near Harvard. I asked some students for directions to where I could find the historic homes built during the 1800s. I was directed to Brattle Street. I soon found a home that was the kind of home where the fictional Fordham Wadsworth Parsons IV might have lived as a child when he adopted neighbor poet Henry Wadsworth Longfellow as one of his two foster grandfathers. I then noticed that the house next to the home I had chosen had indeed belonged to Longfellow and was the place where he died in 1882 when the fictional Fordham was about 9 years old.

I had never been to the Waterbury and Stowe, Vermont, area until after I had completed the first draft of Christmas in Ashton. I was excited as I explored the area the next day and found it to be a perfect fit for the novel I had been working on for the previous 12 years. I revisited the area a year later on Christmas Day in 1997 and was even more convinced that I had chosen the right setting for the fictional village of Ashton, Vermont.

In 1994 I asked my friends, the Lonnie Gunter family, to assist me in the creation of genealogical charts suitable for my novel. Twelve-year-old Lewis Gunter said he could do it. He was assisted by his ten-year-old brother Levin and their father Lonnie. My sister, Peggy Handerhan, typed the first draft of Christmas in Ashton and over the next two years my mother, Peggy K. Williams, and my sister assisted in the first editing of the book.

Since then, countless friends, associates, and family members have read the story and have encouraged me to publish it. Melissa Marler of Precision Editing Group of Salt Lake City helped refine the story, and Julie Lynch Schacht provided the beautiful painting of the Bradford Inn.

I have also been assisted in the publication of this book by Brad Jackman of Shoebox Genealogy, and my son-in-law David N. Miller. Their experience and technical expertise has been instrumental in making this first edition possible. To all these special individuals, I say, "Thank you!"

Kendall H. Williams
November 29, 2013

Additional Notes

It's a Wonderful Life

Frank Capra's "It's a Wonderful Life" was released in 1946, the year of my birth. It starred Jimmy Stewart, who would later become a cherished friend. I later followed the career of golfer Billy Casper as he won the first of his two U.S. Opens in 1959. Fourteen years later, he too became my friend, and remains so even to this day. I watched the Dick Van Dyke television show during the 1960's, and enjoyed the program. Little did I know that comedian Morey Amsterdam who played Buddy Sorell on the show would also become a dear friend. These special friendships were made possible through my career as a professional genealogist.

My life has not been easy, and I have endured many trials and obstacles. I've become acquainted with many wonderful people during my 45 year career in genealogy and family history. I have a lot of wonderful memories of visits with prominent businessmen, entertainers, church leaders, politicians, and individuals who are not famous except to their friends and family. I have witnessed all these wonderful people shed a few tears as

I have told them about their ancestors.

In terms of money, I am not a wealthy man. However, in the things that matter most, I have been richly blessed.

Kendall H. Williams
November 29, 2013

About the Author

Kendall H. Williams

Kendall H. Williams is one of the foremost genealogists in America with over 45 years of research experience, and was instrumental in the creation of both the Federation of Genealogical Societies and the Association of Professional Genealogists. He served a mission for the Church of Jesus Christ of Latter-day Saints to Norway, where he learned the language and grew to love their heritage.

Williams is the author of a family history entitled, "The Syrett Family: From Buckinghamshire, England, to Utah, to Ruby's Inn." He has also co-authored a number of genealogical resource books. In 1983, he wrote and produced a 13-minute video entitled "Welcome Home, Jimmy Stewart," to be shown during the 75th birthday celebration for actor Jimmy Stewart, held in Stewart's hometown of Indiana, Pennsylvania.

Williams has also been commissioned to research the ancestry of many of the world's notable celebrities and business people, including John Wayne, Johnny Carson, Jimmy Stewart, Quincy Jones, Bob Hope, Bing Crosby, Elvis Presley, Richard Pryor, Patrick Wayne, Cheryl Ladd and friend and golf legend, Billy Casper.

Family history has become a hallmark of Williams' life, and his many experiences and discoveries have led him to write this work. Many years in the making, this book is a labor of love tells the remarkable story of a family brought together through family history.

Kendall H. Williams currently resides in Pleasant Grove, Utah.

www.ingramcontent.com/pod-product-compliance
Lightning Source LLC
Chambersburg PA
CBHW070520260626
47161CB00004B/1603